CHARLES & MARY LAMB

Tales from Shakespeare

莎翁故事集

Adaptation and Activities by Silvana Sardi
Illustrated by Alicia Baladan

U0063726

The Commercial Press

Contents 目錄

This Collection of Plays by Shakespeare

As You Like It

Love, adventure and romance for the brave Orlando in the Forest of Arden.

The Merchant of Venice

Antonio the merchant risks death at the hands of his enemy Shylock.

The Tempest

The magic world of Prospero and his fight for justice.

Twelfth Night, or What You Will

Disguise, and confusion over identity, make this love story full of fun.

Macbeth

A man's ambition and his belief in the words of three evil witches lead to death and destruction.

Much Ado About Nothing

Jealous of his half-brother and his friends, Don John plans to ruin the day for all.

A Midsummer Night's Dream

Tiny fairies cause a lot of confusion when they decide to play with the magical love juice from a little purple flower.

An Introduction to Drama

Charles and Mary Lamb wrote a simplified version of Shakespeare's plays in story form in their book *Tales from Shakespeare*. In this collection, these simplified stories have been written as plays again, to be read or acted, maintaining, as the Lambs did, many of Shakespeare's original words. In each play, you'll meet Shakespeare's colourful characters who have to deal with many emotions such as love, hate, ambition and jealousy in many different situations. However, before entering this magical world, it is necessary to understand something about drama in order to fully enjoy Shakespeare's works.

The Origins of Drama and its Elements

Drama is a story, known as a play, acted out on stage, by actors and actresses who take the parts of specific characters. There are two main types: tragedies (serious plays where the main character meets an unhappy end full of disaster) and comedies (funny plays that end happily). The plays are told through dialogue and stage directions which tell the actors how they should move and react to what is happening.

Drama, in its forms of tragedy and comedy, first appeared in the Greek classics. In ancient Greece, people used to gather to watch religious ceremonies. These ceremonies included a **chorus**, a group of people that spoke and moved together, commenting on the main action. From here, drama began to take shape. In any dramatic work, the actors on stage communicate with the audience. Therefore, every performance is different, as the audience can react in a different way. The presentation of the play can also vary, according to the period in which it is shown and the traditions of that time.

Shakespeare's Plays

Shakespeare's plays can be divided into three main types: tragedy, history and comedy plays. In his tragedy plays, the characters are never just ordinary people, but are usually kings or princes and are usually guilty of some action and controlled by fate. Themes usually included in tragedies are suffering, people going mad, and death.

On the other hand, his comedies usually deal with ordinary people in normal situations in an amusing way. There are usually strange circumstances or confusion over identities which lead to funny situations. Love is also usually one of the main themes, and any problems are solved by the end of the play.

Main Characteristics of a Play

Plays are divided into **acts**[1] and each act is divided into **scenes**[2], according to the **plot** which is a series of events connected to each other.

The acts are usually divided as follows:

Act 1: introduction to the plot and characters.

Act 2: development of the plot (rising action) - these events lead to the turning point in the action.

Act 3: turning point – a decisive[3] change that happens in the situation.

Act 4: complications (falling action) – events following the turning point, which lead to the conclusion.

Act 5: denouement, that is, the solving of all problems, the conclusion.

Elizabethan tragedies were usually introduced by a prologue spoken by the chorus to introduce characters to the audience and set the scene. There was also often an epilogue at the end of the play to conclude the story.

Plot: this is the storyline of the play. Charles and Mary Lamb concentrated on the main plot in Shakespeare's plays, when writing their stories, without including the subplots, stories within a story, which are present in all of Shakespeare's works.

1. **acts:** 幕
2. **scenes:** 佈景
3. **decisive:** 關鍵的

Setting: this is the time and place of the action and is communicated to the audience through dialogue and stage directions which also create the mood and emotional strength of the scene.

Stage directions: these are the instructions that the playwright[1] gives to the director and actors as to how the play should be staged. They give information about the setting and maybe how actors should move and what kind of emotions they should show.

Characters: these are the people in the play. There is usually a key person, known as the **protagonist**, the one most involved in the story. This person is not always a hero, or good person, as can be seen in *Macbeth*. Then there is usually the **antagonist** who is the protagonist's main enemy. Some characters are more important in the play than others, so they are considered **main**, while the others are considered **minor**.

Techniques in Drama

Various techniques are used in drama to make it more effective and to give the audience information about characters or events that have not happened on stage. They are as follows:

Dialogue: when two or more characters speak together. Through dialogue, the audience can understand the plot, find out about characters and their relationships and hear about past or future events.

Asides: words spoken by a character, usually to be heard only by the audience and not by the others on stage. These comments let the audience know what the character is really thinking and can also be comical.

Soliloquy: one character is alone on stage and makes a long speech, in which he tells the audience about his thoughts and feelings, his plans for the future, or why he has behaved in a certain way.

Monologue: there are many characters on stage, but just one of them makes a speech which is usually quite long. Unlike a soliloquy and most asides, a monologue is heard by other characters on stage.

1. **playwright:** 劇作家

Grammar for First

1 **Read about Shakespeare and complete the text with one word for each gap.**

William Shakespeare

William Shakespeare was born in Stratford-upon-Avon, in April 1564. He was (**1**)_____ eldest son and was given a good education at his local school, (**2**)_____ he studied classical authors. He married Anne Hathaway, who was eight years older than (**3**)_____, when he was only eighteen, and they had three children. In 1584, he left his home town and went to London to join a drama company. His success was not (**4**)_____ to his acting abilities, but to his way of writing. He soon became the main playwright of one of the (**5**)_____ successful companies of actors in England called the 'Lord Chamberlain's Men'. In 1559, this company built the Globe Theatre, where most of his plays (**6**)_____ performed. The first plays he wrote were historical, then he moved on to comedies full of romance, and finally turned his attention to the great tragedies, (**7**)_____ Macbeth. After many years of success in London, he eventually retired to his home town, where he died at the (**8**)_____ of fifty-two. Only half of his plays were printed during his lifetime. In all his plays, Shakespeare includes people from all social classes, (**9**)_____ princes to servants, and the action often involves family relationships, (**10**)_____ father and child, brother and sister, or husband and wife.

At times, the audience is not just aware (**11**)_____ the action being performed on stage, but is told details of events that have happened off stage, so the play has more depth and meaning. Shakespeare (**12**)_____ use of soliloquies, asides and introductions to give the audience further information necessary to understand the plot and what consequences it has on the characters.

Vocabulary

2 **Look at the introduction and complete the sentences with a word from the box.**

> asides • stage directions • soliloquy • monologue
> plot • turning point

1 Through a _____ the audience and the other actors can find out what a character thinks or feels.

2 _____ are sometimes used to add a comic effect to the scene because the audience knows something that the other characters on stage don't know.

3 An actor knows when to enter a scene by reading the_____.

4 In a _____, an actor has the stage to himself to tell the audience about his thoughts and feelings.

5 The _____is when something important happens in the play that changes all further events.

6 If there is an interesting _____ then the audience will remember the story and will enjoy the play.

Speaking

3 **Discuss and compare with a partner the main features of tragedies and comedies. Think about:**
- characters
- themes
- setting

PRE-READING ACTIVITY

Listening

4 **Listen to the start of the first play in this collection, *As You Like It*. Are these statements true (T) or false (F)?**

	T	F
1 All of France is ruled by one prince.	☐	☐
2 Prince Frederick has an older brother.	☐	☐
3 Arden is the name of the prince's palace.	☐	☐
4 Rosalind and Celia are sisters.	☐	☐
5 Celia wants Rosalind to feel happy.	☐	☐
6 Rosalind is enthusiastic about the idea of a fight.	☐	☐

As You Like It

Characters:

THE PRINCE, *banished[1] from his kingdom.*

ROSALIND, *the Prince's only daughter.*

FREDERICK, *the Prince's younger brother.*

CELIA, *Frederick's daughter.*

ORLANDO, *Sir Rowland de Boys' youngest son.*

OLIVER, *Orlando's eldest brother.*

ADAM, *Sir Rowland de Boys' old servant.*

CORIN, *an old man living in the Forest of Arden.*

CHARLES, *a fighter.*

SERVANTS.

Many years ago, France was divided into kingdoms, each ruled by a prince. In one such kingdom however, the real prince had been banished by his younger brother, Frederick, who had taken his place. The banished prince now lived with his loyal friends in the Forest of Arden, where they enjoyed the simple life. His daughter, Rosalind, who had been forced to stay in the kingdom without her father, had become good friends with Celia, Frederick's daughter. Rosalind was often sad because she missed her father, but Celia always tried to entertain her.

1. banished: 流放

Act 1 Scene 1

France. Outside the Prince's Palace.

[*Enter Rosalind and Celia.*]

CELIA. Please, my sweet cousin, Rosalind, be cheerful.

ROSALIND. Dear Celia, how can I be happy when I miss my father so much?

[*Enter servant.*]

SERVANT. Mistress Celia, there is a match about to start.

CELIA. What kind of match?

SERVANT. Two men who must fight each other.

CELIA. Come, Rosalind. Maybe a good fight will lift your spirits.

ROSALIND. If you say so, dear cousin.

[*Exit all.*]

Act 1 Scene 2

Palace grounds.

[*Enter Prince Frederick, Celia, Rosalind and the two fighters. One, called Charles, is very big and strong, while the other is just a young boy who seems much weaker.*]

ROSALIND. Must the boy fight against that huge man?

CELIA. Oh dear! He's far too young.

FREDERICK. The boy has no chance of winning, but won't listen to reason. Maybe if you speak to him, ladies, he'll give up the fight. Come Charles, my good man; we must speak together.

[*Exit Frederick and Charles.*]

CELIA. Young gentleman, you have too much courage for your age. Please, for your own safety, give up this challenge.

ROSALIND. Do, young sir; your good name won't be damaged.

ORLANDO. Let your kind eyes and gentle wishes go with me to my challenge. If I'm defeated, I'll do my friends no wrong, for I have none to cry for me; only a brother who hates me.

ROSALIND. Then, be strong and quick.

[*Re-enter Frederick and Charles with servants.*]

CHARLES. Are you ready, young man?

ORLANDO. Ready, sir.

CHARLES. You'll only last one fall.

ORLANDO. We'll see.

[*Charles and Orlando fight. Charles is thrown to the ground.*]

ROSALIND. Oh excellent young man!

FREDERICK. No more, no more. [*to servants*] Take Charles away.

[*Exit Charles, helped by servants.*]

FREDERICK. What's your name, young man?

ORLANDO. Orlando, my lord; the youngest son of Sir Rowland de Boys.

FREDERICK. The world judged your father as a man of honour; for me, he was an enemy. You did well and you're a fine youth, but I'd have been better pleased if you had told me of another father.

[*Exit Prince Frederick.*]

ORLANDO. I'm proud to be Sir Rowland's son.

ROSALIND. My father loved Sir Rowland.

CELIA. Sir, my father's unkind words strike my heart. You deserve only to be praised.

ROSALIND. Gentleman, [*giving him a chain from her neck.*] wear this for me; if I were richer, I'd give you more.

CELIA. Shall we go, cousin?

ROSALIND. Goodbye, fine gentleman.

[*Exit Rosalind and Celia.*]

ORLANDO. What passion ties my tongue? I didn't speak to her, yet she was waiting for my answer. Oh poor Orlando! You've been beaten, not by Charles, but by another weakness.

[*Enter servant.*]

SERVANT. Good sir, I advise you to leave this place. Prince Frederick is turning everyone against you.

ORLANDO. I thank you, sir; but please, tell me; which of the two ladies is the prince's daughter?

SERVANT. In manners neither; but indeed, the smaller is his daughter: the other is daughter to the banished prince. They are like sisters to each other. But lately, Prince Frederick has turned against his gentle niece; the people praise her good qualities, and feel sorry for her, because of her father's situation. One day, for sure, he'll try to harm the poor girl. Goodbye sir; may you find a better world than this.

ORLANDO. Goodbye and thank you once more, my friend.

[*Exit servant.*]

ORLANDO. So I must go from a terrible prince back to my terrible brother, Oliver. Despite him being the eldest, and the promises made to my dead father, Oliver has no care of me and gives me nothing but misery. No education, no love. Oh, but sweet Rosalind!

[*Exit Orlando.*]

Act 1 Scene 3

A room in the Palace.

[*Enter Celia and Rosalind.*]

CELIA. Why, Rosalind! Not a word? Is all this for your father?

ROSALIND. Just some of it.

CELIA. Can it be, that so suddenly, you should fall in love with Sir Rowland's youngest son?

ROSALIND. The Prince, my father, loved his father dearly.

CELIA. Does that mean you should love his son dearly? In that case, I should hate him, for my father hated his father; yet I hate not Orlando.

ROSALIND. No, please don't hate him. I love him. Look, here comes your father.

CELIA. With his eyes full of anger.

[*Enter Prince Frederick.*]

FREDERICK. Mistress, get your things ready and leave this palace immediately.

ROSALIND. Me, uncle?

FREDERICK. Yes, you; be gone from my palace forever, or die.

ROSALIND. I beg you, my lord, tell me what fault I have.

FREDERICK. I don't trust you.

ROSALIND. Why not?

FREDERICK. You are your father's daughter. That is good enough reason.

CELIA. Please, father, hear me speak. When you sent her father away, I didn't ask you to let Rosalind stay. I was too young then. But, now I know her; if you don't trust her, then you can't trust me either. We can't be separated.

FREDERICK. She does you wrong. Her silence and patience make people feel pity for her. You'll shine brighter once she has gone. Say no more; my decision is made; she must leave.

[*Exit Prince Frederick.*]

CELIA. Oh my poor Rosalind! Where will you go?

ROSALIND. I know not.

CELIA. We won't be separated. Help me to plan our escape.

ROSALIND. But where shall we go?

CELIA. To the Forest of Arden, to look for my uncle.

ROSALIND. But it's dangerous there, especially for two ladies like us. Maybe it'd be better if I dressed as a man from the countryside; I'm taller than usual for a woman.

CELIA. And I'll be your sister and wear the poor clothes of a village girl. But, what will I call you when you're a man?

ROSALIND. Call me Ganymede. And you? What will you be called?

CELIA. Aliena. Right, let's get our wealth together. We'll leave this night.

[*Exit all.*]

Act 2 Scene 1

In front of Oliver's house.

[*Enter Orlando and Adam, once, his father's loyal servant.*]

ADAM. Oh my sweet, young master. You're so like your dear father, Sir Rowland. How are you so strong, yet gentle? Why did you win against Prince Frederick's man? News of this win has already arrived before you and goes against you.

ORLANDO. Why?

ADAM. Oh, my poor boy! Your eldest brother, Oliver, planned the fight, thinking you wouldn't survive. He's always been jealous of the fact that you have your father's good nature and elegant manners. Now he's furious, and plans to burn this house while you're sleeping in it, this night. Run away, Orlando!

ORLANDO. But where will I go? Will I live on the road and have to beg for food or steal? No! I'd rather face my evil brother.

ADAM. Take these five hundred gold coins; all I have. I'll come with you and be your servant. Despite my age, I promise to be as loyal to you, as I was to your father.

ORLANDO. Oh good old man! We'll go together then, and leave this dreadful place forever.

[*Exit all.*]

Act 2 Scene 2

The Forest of Arden.

[*Enter Rosalind in boy's clothes and Celia dressed as a village girl.*]

ROSALIND. Oh, how tired I am! Were it not for these boy's clothes, I'd cry like a woman. Instead, I must help the weaker one, as men do; so courage, good Aliena.

CELIA. I'm sorry; I can't go any further.

ROSALIND. Well, this is the Forest of Arden. Look! An old man is coming our way.

CELIA. Ask him, if he has any food.

[*Enter Corin, an old man.*]

ROSALIND. Good evening to you, my friend.

CORIN. And to you, gentle sir.

ROSALIND. Please, kind friend; my young sister is exhausted with travelling and ready to faint with hunger.

CORIN. Kind sir, I'm sorry, and wish that I had more to give; but I'm a shepherd[1] and my master is not generous. He's away now, and his house is empty and is to be sold, but you're welcome to come and rest there.

ROSALIND. We'll buy the cottage and the sheep.

CELIA. And we'll pay you to work for us.

CORIN. Come then; if you like what you see, and this kind of life, then it'll be yours.

ROSALIND [*aside to Celia*]. Good fortune! We can stay in the cottage until we find my father in the forest.

[*Exit all.*]

Act 2 Scene 3

Another part of the Forest of Arden.

[*Enter Orlando and Adam.*]

ADAM. Dear master, I can go no further; hunger has eaten my strength. Let me lie down here and die.

ORLANDO. Courage Adam! Rest here under these trees, while I hunt for some food I'll be back soon.

[*Exit Orlando.*]

Act 2 Scene 4

Another part of the forest.

[*The banished Prince is sitting on the grass, eating with some friends.*]

PRINCE. Come my friends; let's eat and be grateful for what we

---

1. **shepherd:** 牧羊人

have. But who comes here?

[*Enter Orlando with his sword.*]

ORLANDO. Eat no more!

PRINCE. I have eaten nothing yet.

ORLANDO. And you won't start until my need has been served.

PRINCE. Is it despair that makes you rude, young man?

ORLANDO. I almost die for food.

PRINCE. Then, sit down and eat; welcome to our table.

ORLANDO. Speak you so gently? I thought all things here were wild. If ever you've looked on better days, and know what pity is, then please forgive me.

PRINCE. 'True is it that we have seen better days.' So, in kindness, sit down and tell us how we can help you.

ORLANDO. First, I must feed a poor old man who has served me with love.

PRINCE. Go and get him; we'll wait for your return.

ORLANDO. Thank you, my lord!

[*Exit Orlando.*]

PRINCE. We aren't the only ones on this earth who have been unhappy. 'All the world's a stage, and all the men and women merely players.'

[*Re-enter Orlando carrying Adam.*]

PRINCE. Welcome; sit the man down and let him eat.

ORLANDO. I thank you most for him.

ADAM. I can hardly speak to thank you for myself.

PRINCE. Young boy, you remind me of my dear friend, Sir Rowland de Boys.

ORLANDO. I'm his youngest son.

PRINCE. Then, you're most welcome. I'm the Prince, whose brother Frederick, banished to this forest. I loved your father dearly. We'll look after you and your friend. After eating, you must rest.

ORLANDO. Thank you, my lord.

[*Exit all.*]

Act 3 Scene 1

The Forest of Arden

[*Enter Orlando with a paper.*]

ORLANDO. Hang there my poem, witness of my love. Oh Rosalind! These trees will be my books, where I'll carve[1] my thoughts for everyone in the forest to see.

[*Exit Orlando.*]

[*Enter Rosalind reading a paper.*]

ROSALIND. *'From east to west, no jewel is like Rosalind.*
Let no face be kept in mind, but that of my sweet love.'

ROSALIND. I wonder who has written these words that I found hanging on a bush.

[*Enter Celia reading a paper.*]

CELIA. *'On every tree, Rosalind's name will I write,*
So this place, no longer a desert, but will be bright,
with tongues speaking of Rosalind through the night.'

CELIA. Rosalind, have you read these words?

ROSALIND. Yes, I've found many papers hanging on branches and bushes, and many other words carved on the trees themselves.

CELIA. Who has written such messages of love? But hush! Here comes a young man.

[*Enter Orlando.*]

CELIA [*aside to Rosalind*]. A young man 'and a chain that you once wore, about his neck'. It's Orlando, who with the fight, won your heart.

ROSALIND [*aside to Celia*]. He doesn't recognise us; I'll speak to him as man to man.

ROSALIND [*to Orlando*]. Good sir, please tell me what time it is.

1. carve: 刻

ORLANDO. There's no clock in the forest. Where do you live young man?

ROSALIND. With my sister in the shepherd's cottage on the edge of the forest. There may be no clock, but there's a lazy lover who sighs every minute of the day in this forest. He's ruining all the trees by carving 'Rosalind' on them; not only that, he hangs poems everywhere, on plants and bushes. If I met that young man, I'd give him some good advice because he seems to be love-sick.

ORLANDO. I am he that is so love-sick. Please tell me your cure. It's strange, but in some ways you seem like my Rosalind, though you lack her delicate manners.

ROSALIND. Are you so love-sick, that you see your Rosalind everywhere? Are you as much in love as your poems speak?

ORLANDO. Even more than any words can say.

ROSALIND. Love is like madness, but with my help, I'm sure I can cure you of this illness.

ORLANDO. How? Please tell me.

ROSALIND. You must imagine that I'm your love, Rosalind; every day you'll come to win my heart with sweet romantic words. You'll call me Rosalind and I'll pretend to be the woman of your dreams. One day I'll love you, the next I'll hate you; then I'll cry for you, and then again I'll be angry with you. In this way you'll see how a woman can change her mind so easily, and your heart will be washed clean of any signs of love.

ORLANDO. I'll try. Tell me where your cottage is. I'll come every day.

ROSALIND. Come with me and my sister, and I'll show you.

[*Exit all.*]

Act 4 Scene 1

The Forest of Arden.

[*Enter Celia and Rosalind.*]

ROSALIND. Don't talk to me; I'll cry.

CELIA. Remember, men don't cry.

ROSALIND. But have I not the right to cry?

CELIA. Yes; so, cry if you must.

ROSALIND. Why did he promise to come, then didn't?

CELIA. Maybe there's no truth in your Orlando.

ROSALIND. But you heard him say he was in love.

CELIA. Sometimes the promise of a lover isn't strong. Maybe he's serving your father in this forest.

ROSALIND. I met my father yesterday. He asked me what kind of family I came from; I answered one as good as his. He laughed and let me go. Enough of my father; Orlando is more important at the moment.

CELIA. Yes, brave Orlando, with his brave words of love. Here he is now.

[*Enter Orlando.*]

ORLANDO. Good day, and happiness, dear Rosalind!

ROSALIND. Why, how now, Orlando! Where have you been all this time? You a lover! You've tricked me. Never show your face to me again.

ORLANDO. My sweet Rosalind; it's hardly past the hour of my promise to come.

ROSALIND. You've broken your promise. You're late; come no more.

ORLANDO. Please forgive me, dear Rosalind.

ROSALIND. Now I'm of good humour. What would you say to me now if I really were your Rosalind?

ORLANDO. I'd kiss before I spoke.

ROSALIND. No, you'd better speak first; then if you've no more words to say, you can kiss. But, now I'll pretend to be your Rosalind with an even sweeter nature. Ask me whatever you want.

ORLANDO. Then, love me, Rosalind.

ROSALIND. Yes, I will, every day.

ORLANDO. And will you marry me?

ROSALIND. Yes. Come sister, you'll pretend to be the priest and marry us. Give me your hand Orlando. What do you say, Aliena?

CELIA. Will you, Orlando, have Rosalind as your wife?

ORLANDO. I will.

ROSALIND. But when?

ORLANDO. Why now; as fast as she can marry us.

ROSALIND. Now, tell me Orlando, how long would you stay with your Rosalind after you were married?

ORLANDO. For ever and a day.

ROSALIND. No, Orlando; the sky changes for men when they take a wife. So, I'll be a jealous wife. I'll cry for nothing when you're happy. Then I'll laugh when you're feeling sad.

ORLANDO. But will my Rosalind do so?

ROSALIND. 'By my life, she will do as I do.'

ORLANDO. Oh! But she is wise.

ROSALIND. Or else she wouldn't have the sense of humour to do this.

ORLANDO. For two hours I must leave you, Rosalind. I have to serve the prince at dinner.

ROSALIND. Remember; don't break your promise by being late.

ORLANDO. I'll be here on time, as if you were really my Rosalind.

ROSALIND. Goodbye till then.

[*Exit Orlando.*]

ROSALIND. I'm so in love that 'I cannot be out of the sight of Orlando: I'll go find a shadow and sigh till he come'.

CELIA. And I'll sleep.

[*Exit all.*]

Act 4 Scene 2

The Forest of Arden.

[*Enter Rosalind and Celia.*]

ROSALIND. More than two hours have gone and Orlando isn't to be seen.

CELIA. Maybe he's hunting.

[*Enter Oliver with handkerchief stained with blood.*]

OLIVER. Good day. Can you tell me where the shepherd's cottage is?

CELIA. It's west of here.

OLIVER. Are you by chance the owners of the cottage?

CELIA. Yes, indeed.

OLIVER. Orlando sends me to greet you both, and to the youth he calls Rosalind, he sends this bloody handkerchief. Are you he?

ROSALIND. I am: what must be understood by this?

OLIVER. While Orlando was walking through the forest, he saw a man sleeping on the ground: around this man's neck was a green, poisonous snake with its mouth open, ready to bite; but suddenly it saw Orlando and slipped away into the bushes. Then, behind this bush was a lion, lying low, ready to attack. When Orlando approached the man to warn him of the danger, he realised that it was me, his brother Oliver.

CELIA. Oh! So you are the brother that hates him?

OLIVER. Not anymore; but I'm ashamed to say I've been a cruel and unnatural brother.

ROSALIND. So, what did Orlando do?

OLIVER. Twice, he turned his back as if to go away; then kindness, stronger than revenge, made him fight the lion in my defence. Then we hugged and I felt shame for my past actions but happiness for the love of my dear brother.

ROSALIND. But, this bloody handkerchief?

OLIVER. After defeating the lion, Orlando took me to the prince in this forest. Only then did he realise the lion had bitten his arm; he had, by now, bled for so long that he fainted, crying out the name Rosalind. He's still weak and has sent me to you, so that you may forgive him for his delay.

CELIA [*Rosalind faints*]. Ganymede!

OLIVER. Many faint at the sight of blood.

CELIA. There's more in it. Ganymede!

ROSALIND. Take me home.

CELIA [*to Oliver*]. Can you take him by the arm?

OLIVER. Young man, you lack a man's heart.

ROSALIND. Tell your brother I pretended to faint for him, as his Rosalind would have done.

OLIVER. You seem very pale to be pretending.

CELIA. Good sir, please help me take him home.

OLIVER. That I will.

[*Exit all.*]

Act 5 Scene 1

The Forest of Arden.

[*Enter Orlando and Oliver.*]

ORLANDO. Is it possible that you love her already, and Aliena loves you?

OLIVER. We neither understand; we know only that we both love each other dearly. All that I have, I give to you, dear brother. I'll live happily in this forest with my shepherd girl.

ORLANDO. Then let your wedding be tomorrow, and I'll invite the prince of the forest and his friends. Go and tell Aliena, for here comes my Rosalind.

[*Enter Rosalind.*]

ROSALIND. Good day, brother.

OLIVER. And to you too.

[*Exit Oliver.*]

ROSALIND. Oh my dear Orlando! How sorry I am to see you injured. Did your brother tell you how I pretended to faint?

ORLANDO. Yes and more.

ROSALIND. Ah, yes! Your brother and my sister – love at first sight! Isn't it amazing?

OLIVER. They'll be married tomorrow, and I'll invite the prince to their wedding. 'How bitter a thing it is to look into happiness through another man's eyes'. I can bear no longer to pretend you are my Rosalind.

ROSALIND. I know you're a good man, and I want to help you. I can do strange things, as I've an uncle who taught me magic when I was a child. If you really love Rosalind as you say, then tomorrow, when your brother marries Aliena, you'll find Rosalind waiting for you to become your wife.

OLIVER. Do you mean what you say?

ROSALIND. By my life, I do. So, put on your best clothes, and go and tell your friends you're to be married to Rosalind tomorrow. I must go to my sister.

[*Exit all.*]

Act 5 Scene 2

Another part of the forest.

[*Enter the banished prince, Orlando, Oliver and Celia.*]

PRINCE. Do you really believe, Orlando, that the boy can do all he says?

ORLANDO. Sometimes yes, and sometimes no.

[*Enter Rosalind.*]

ROSALIND [*to prince*]. If I bring your Rosalind here, will you let her marry Orlando?

PRINCE. That I will.

ROSALIND [*to Orlando*]. And will you have her when I bring her?

ORLANDO. That I will.

ROSALIND. I've promised to make all this happen. Keep your word, my lords, and all will be well.

[*Exit Rosalind and Celia.*]

PRINCE. There's something about this shepherd-boy that reminds me of my daughter.

ORLANDO. My lord, the first time I saw him, I thought he was a brother to your daughter. But this boy has always lived in the forest.

[*Enter Rosalind and Celia both dressed as elegant women.*]

ROSALIND [*to prince*]. To you I give myself, for I'm yours, dear father and there's no magic. I was banished like you, and kind Celia, here, came with me. I dressed as a country boy, and Celia as my sister; we came to this forest where we've been staying in the shepherd's cottage.

PRINCE. Oh my dear daughter! My dear niece!

ORLANDO. My dearest Rosalind!

ROSALIND [*to Orlando*]. I'll have no husband, if you be not he.

PRINCE [*to Orlando and Rosalind*]. You and you will never part [*to Celia and Oliver.*] You and you are heart in heart. Let's proceed with this double wedding.

[*Enter servant.*]

SERVANT. My lord and my prince, I have news for you. Prince Frederick, on hearing how many men had decided to live in the forest with you, was on his way here with his army to challenge you. However, just as he reached the edge of forest, he met an old wise man, who convinced Frederick to change his ways and become a good man. He'll attack no more, and you are, once again, Prince of your kingdom.

CELIA. Oh great joy! My dear uncle, you are prince once more and you, sweet Rosalind, will have his kingdom one day.

ROSALIND. Dear cousin, sweet Celia, your kindness shows no regret for your loss.

CELIA. I'm happy enough that my father has become a wiser man and done the right thing at last.

PRINCE [*to servant*]. I thank you for this joyful news, and promise that all those who've been loyal to me, will have their lands and homes once more. Let's go now and celebrate this double wedding with even more joy in our hearts.

[*Exit all.*]

Stop & Check

1 Use the clues below to complete the crossword about *As You Like It*.

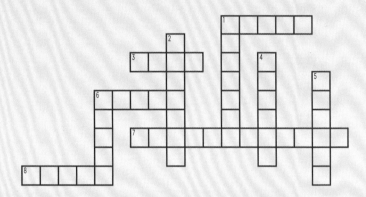

Clues Across

1 Rosalind gives this to Orlando after the fight.

3 Orlando hangs this on a tree to show his love for Rosalind.

6 Orlando is ready to fight the prince for food with this.

7 Oliver brings this to Rosalind with a message from Orlando.

8 Rosalind was taught magic by this person.

Clues Down

1 Rosalind and Celia buy this to live in.

2 At the end of the play there is this kind of celebration.

4 The country where the play is set.

5 The place where the banished prince lives.

6 Oliver is nearly bitten by this animal.

Grammar for First

2 Complete the second sentence so that it means the same as the first. Use between two and five words, including the word given, without changing it.

1 Oliver didn't let Orlando have an education.
allowed
Orlando _____ have an education.

2 Only Frederick hated Sir Rowland.
except
Everyone _____ Frederick.

3 When everyone saw Charles, they had no doubts that he'd win against Orlando.
chance
Everyone thought that Orlando _____ against Charles.

4 The last time the prince saw Rosalind, was before he was sent to the forest.
seen
The prince _____ being sent to the forest.

5 Adam was so tired and hungry that he had to lie down.
too
Adam was _____ walk anymore.

PRE-READING ACTIVITY

Listening

3 Listen to Act 1 Scene 1 of the next play, *The Merchant of Venice*, and answer the following questions.

1 Why does Bassanio think Portia might love him?
2 Why has Portia suddenly become rich?
3 Why does Bassanio want to borrow money from Antonio?
4 Why can't Antonio satisfy his friend immediately?
5 Why can't Bassanio wait a bit?
6 How do they decide to solve the problem?

29

The Merchant[1] of Venice

Characters:

GOVERNOR OF VENICE.
SHYLOCK, *rich moneylender.*
ANTONIO, *merchant from Venice.*
BASSANIO, *Antonio's friend.*
PORTIA, *a rich lady.*
GRATIANO, *Bassanio's friend.*
NERISSA, *Portia's servant.*
SERVANT.

Antonio, a young, generous merchant from Venice, is known and liked by everybody, except Shylock, a Jew, and rich moneylender. Antonio's best friend, Bassanio, a young gentleman, always has money problems, so often asks his friend Antonio to help him.

Act 1 Scene 1

A street in Venice.

[Enter Antonio and Bassanio.]

ANTONIO. Well, Bassanio, you promised to tell me about a pretty lady you admire.

1. merchant: 商人

BASSANIO. As you know, my dear Antonio, my fortune is nearly all gone; but now I have a plan to solve all my money problems, and this lady is part of it.

ANTONIO. Please, tell me more.

BASSANIO. In Belmont, there's a beautiful lady called Portia. I often visited her in the past, and am sure that her eyes sent me messages of love. Her beauty is known all over the world, and now that she's also become wealthy since the death of her father, many men wish to marry her. I dearly love this sweet lady, but Portia deserves a man of elegant appearance, who can give her many gifts.

ANTONIO. You know, dear friend, that all my fortunes are at sea at the moment. I'm waiting for my three ships full of merchandise[1] to arrive soon in Venice.

BASSANIO. But I need the money now, to go to Belmont, otherwise another man will steal Portia's heart.

ANTONIO. Then, we'll find someone to borrow the money from, and I'll look after all costs. They'll trust me, as they know I'm a good merchant and have three ships.

BASSANIO. Thank you, my dear friend.

[*Exit all.*]

Act 1 Scene 2

Venice. A public place.

[*Enter Bassanio and Shylock.*]

SHYLOCK. So, you want three thousand gold coins for three months, right?

BASSANIO. Yes sir; and as I said, Antonio will be responsible for the amount lent.

SHYLOCK. Antonio is a good man. But I'm a little worried that he might not have enough money.

BASSANIO. But he has three ships full of merchandise.

---

1. merchandise: 商品

SHYLOCK. But the ships are at sea, and there are many dangers, like storms, pirates and so on. I need to be assured that he can respect our agreement.

BASSANIO. Look! Here he comes now.

[*Enter Antonio.*]

BASSANIO. Antonio! Here you are!

SHYLOCK [*aside*]. I hate him; he always lends money without making people pay extra for this service. He spoils business for all moneylenders in Venice like me.

BASSANIO. Shylock?

SHYLOCK. I was thinking about how much money I have ready.

ANTONIO. I don't usually ask anyone for money, but I'd do anything for my dear friend, Bassanio.

SHYLOCK. Many times in the past, you've insulted me, Antonio, because I make people pay for borrowing money from me; but this is my way of business. Now it seems you need my help. Why should I lend you money now, when you've called me a dog so many times?

ANTONIO. Because it's better for you to lend your money to an enemy than to a friend; for if your enemy can't pay, you can better punish him, than if he were a friend.

SHYLOCK. Why all this anger? I'd like to be your friend. I'll lend you the money at no extra cost, as a sign of my kindness.

ANTONIO [*surprised*]. That would truly be kindness.

SHYLOCK. So, let's go to a lawyer where we'll sign our agreement; and just for fun, we'll also write that if you don't give me the money back after three months, then you'll give me a pound[1] of your flesh[2] to be cut from any part of your body, as pleases me.

ANTONIO. So be it!

BASSANIO. No, Antonio! I won't let you sign such an agreement for me.

ANTONIO. Don't worry, my friend. We have three months to pay.

SHYLOCK. Bassanio, sir, why don't you trust me? Do you really think

---

1. pound: 一磅，約0.45公斤   **2. flesh:** 肉

I want a pound of this man's flesh? What would I do with such a thing? A pound of beef would be worth more. I was only trying to help you, but if you don't want my friendship, then….

ANTONIO. Shylock, I accept your kind offer and will sign our agreement.

SHYLOCK. Excellent! Let's meet at the lawyer's and sign the document.

[*Exit Shylock.*]

BASSANIO. I don't like you having an agreement with this evil man.

ANTONIO. Don't worry; my ships will be here a month before we have to pay. Meanwhile, you can buy all you need to win your sweet lady's heart.

BASSANIO. Yes, my dear friend; and then I'll be rich enough to pay our debts.

[*Exit all.*]

Act 2 Scene 1

Belmont. A room in Portia's house.

[*Enter Portia and Nerissa.*]

NERISSA. My lady, there is a young man from Venice at your gate with his handsome friend, an elegant gentleman, who has brought many gifts.

PORTIA. Bring him to me.

NERISSA [*aside*]. It is Bassanio; I recognised him. Many times my dear mistress has enjoyed his company. She'll surely be pleased, and I too, will be happy to see his friend.

[*Exit Nerissa.*]

PORTIA. While my father was still alive, a young man from Venice used to pay me visit; Bassanio was his name. Could it be him? I have fond memories of him.

[*Enter Nerissa with Bassanio and Gratiano.*]

BASSANIO. My dearest Portia; I'm not worthy of the attention of a lady as sweet and beautiful as yourself. I'm not a rich man, and can only offer you the good name of my family.

PORTIA. For myself alone, I wouldn't be ambitious; yet for you, I wish to be a thousand times more beautiful, and ten thousand times richer, in order to deserve your love and respect. My wealth, beauty and friends have no value when you consider that I lack knowledge and practice. My only quality is my young age, which gives me plenty of time to learn. Yesterday I was queen of myself; now 'this house, these servants, and this same myself are yours, my lord. I give them with this ring'. However, if you ever lose this ring or give it away, it'll mean that our love has died.

BASSANIO. Madam, I'm lost for words. I can't believe that a lady as sweet as you, can accept a man like myself as her husband; a man who has nothing to offer, but his love. I thank you for this ring and promise, it'll never leave my finger.

NERISSA. My lord and lady, good joy!

GRATIANO. My Lord Bassanio and my gentle lady, I wish you every happiness. May I be married the same time as you?

BASSANIO. Of course! If you can find a wife.

GRATIANO. I thank you, my lord, for I already have one. While your eyes fell on the mistress of the house, I fell in love with her servant, Nerissa, who has promised to be my wife.

PORTIA. Is this true Nerissa?

NERISSA. Madam, it is.

BASSANIO. A double wedding will be a joyful event.

GRATIANO. Thank you my lord. But, look! Here comes someone with a letter.

[*Enter servant with letter in hand.*]

SERVANT. Bassanio, my lord; a letter for you from Venice.

BASSANIO. I recognise the writing; it's from my dear friend, Antonio.
[*Opens the letter and starts reading.*]

PORTIA. What's wrong Bassanio? Your face is pale; is it bad news?

BASSANIO. Oh sweet Portia! When I told you I had nothing, my situation was actually worse than nothing. I borrowed money from my dear friend, Antonio, and he signed an agreement with a moneylender, by which he took entire responsibility for the payment. He was sure that there would be no problems as he was waiting for three of his ships to arrive full of merchandise.

PORTIA. So why does this letter make you suffer so?

BASSANIO. Because Antonio has lost all three ships at sea, and now Shylock, the cruel moneylender, demands a pound of Antonio's flesh as payment.

PORTIA. But this is impossible.

BASSANIO. Unfortunately, Shylock has every right, because it is written in the agreement Antonio signed. Antonio asks me to go to him before he dies by paying this debt. Oh my poor friend! It's all my fault.

PORTIA. Hush, my dear! How much must he give the moneylender?

BASSANIO. Three thousand gold coins.

PORTIA. Is that all? Pay him six thousand and break the agreement. Or even twelve or eighteen! As long as your friend is safe, Bassanio. First marry me, so you'll have legal right to my fortune; then go with Gratiano to Venice, to your friend. When the debt is paid, bring your friend back here. Meanwhile, Nerissa and I will wait impatiently for your return.

BASSANIO. Thank you, my love. Come, Gratiano; let's go to the church to marry our sweet wives, then on to Venice.

[*Exit all.*]

Act 3 Scene 1

Belmont. A room in Portia's house.

[*Enter Portia and Nerissa.*]

PORTIA. Nerissa, tell that new servant to take this letter to my cousin, the lawyer, Doctor Bellario, in Padua. Doctor Bellario will give the boy some clothes and notes for us. Then, he should meet us at the ferry that goes to Venice.

NERISSA. I don't understand, mistress; are we going to Venice?

PORTIA. Yes, we'll see our husbands before they think about us.

NERISSA. Will they see us?

PORTIA. Yes, but we'll be dressed as men, so they won't recognise us.

NERISSA. But why must we dress as men?

PORTIA. I'll tell you everything on the way to Venice. Come now; we must get there in time to speak in Antonio's defence.

[*Exit all.*]

Act 4 Scene 1

Venice. High Court of Justice.

[*Enter the Governor of Venice, Antonio, Bassanio and Gratiano.*]

GOVERNOR. Is Antonio here?

ANTONIO. I'm here and ready, sir.

GOVERNOR. I'm sorry for you and your case against such a cruel moneylender, who feels no pity.

ANTONIO. Since the law can find no fault with his case, I must patiently accept the consequences.

[*Enter Shylock.*]

GOVERNOR. Come and stand before us. Shylock, the world thinks, and I too, that in the end, you'll have pity on this man, Antonio, and won't demand your pound of flesh. Since he's lost all his ships, you'll forgive him for not paying you on time. Please give us a gentle answer, sir.

SHYLOCK. I don't intend to change my mind. You can't deny me what is mine by law. I refuse to justify my choice. Let's just say it's my sense of humour, and that I hate this man, Antonio. Is that a good enough answer for you?

BASSANIO. That's no answer; it's no excuse for your cruelty.

SHYLOCK. I'm not here to please you with my answer.

BASSANIO. Do all men kill the things they don't love?

SHYLOCK. Does any man hate the thing he wouldn't kill?

ANTONIO. It's useless, Bassanio. The man has a hard heart.

BASSANIO. I'll give you six thousand gold coins, Shylock.

SHYLOCK. I want what is written in the agreement, that's all; no more, no less.

GOVERNOR. You can expect no pity, if you show none.

SHYLOCK. I have done no wrong; I don't need to be forgiven. The pound of flesh which I demand of him, has been paid for well. If you deny me, then you're breaking the laws of Venice. So, shall I have it?

GOVERNOR. I'm waiting to hear Doctor Bellario's opinion on this case. Has he not arrived yet?

GRATIANO. My lord, there's a gentleman outside with documents from the doctor.

GOVERNOR. Tell him to come in.

BASSANIO. Courage, Antonio! Hope some more!

[*Enter Nerissa, dressed as a lawyer's assistant. No-one recognises her.*]

GOVERNOR. Do you come from Padua, young man? From Bellario?

NERISSA. From both. This letter is for you, my lord.

BASSANIO. Shylock, why are you looking at your knife so carefully?

SHYLOCK. To see if it's sharp enough.

GRATIANO. How can you be so cruel?

SHYLOCK. I stand here with the law.

GOVERNOR. This letter from Bellario says he has sent us a young, brilliant lawyer. Where is he?

NERISSA. Here he is now.

[*Enter Portia dressed as a lawyer. No-one recognises her either.*]

GOVERNOR. Have you come from old Bellario?

PORTIA. I have, my lord. My name is Balthasar.

GOVERNOR. You're welcome, young man. Do you know about this case?

PORTIA. Yes, I've been well-informed. Who's the merchant and who's the moneylender?

GOVERNOR. Antonio and Shylock; step forward!

PORTIA. Is your name Shylock?

SHYLOCK. Shylock is my name.

PORTIA. Your case is of a strange nature, but by the law of Venice, you have the right to have what you demand. [to Antonio.] You're the one in danger, is that correct?

ANTONIO. It seems so.

PORTIA. Do you confess to[1] the agreement?

ANTONIO. I do.

PORTIA. Then the moneylender must have pity.

SHYLOCK. Why should I?

PORTIA. He who shows pity, is greater than any king. Remember this, Shylock, even if you have the law of Venice on your side.

SHYLOCK. I love the law. I want what is written in the agreement.

PORTIA. Is he not able to pay you?

BASSANIO. Yes, I have the money here. I'll pay him twice the amount; if that's not enough, I'll give him ten times more. Please, I beg of you, stop this cruel devil.

PORTIA. It cannot be. There's no power in Venice that can change an existing law.

SHYLOCK. What a wise young man!

PORTIA. Please, let me see the agreement.

SHYLOCK. Here it is, sir.

PORTIA. Shylock, you've been offered more than the amount you lent.

SHYLOCK. I've promised to respect the agreement.

PORTIA. It's written that you can, by law, cut off the pound of

1. confess to: 承認

flesh nearest the merchant's heart. Have pity Shylock! Accept the money, and let me destroy the agreement.

SHYLOCK. You can destroy it, once the debt written on it has been paid. You know the law. Please, declare your judgement.

ANTONIO. Yes, please let the court make its judgement.

PORTIA. Why then, this is it; Antonio, you must prepare your chest for his knife.

SHYLOCK. Oh, true judge! Oh excellent, young man!

PORTIA. Is there something to weigh the flesh?

SHYLOCK. I have it ready.

PORTIA. Shylock, have you got a doctor to stop him bleeding to death?

SHYLOCK. Does it say so in the agreement?

PORTIA. It isn't expressed, but it'd be good if you were to do it out of kindness.

SHYLOCK. I can't find it; it isn't in the agreement.

PORTIA. You, merchant, have you anything to say?

ANTONIO. But little: I'm well prepared. Give me your hand Bassanio; goodbye my friend. Tell your beautiful wife about me. Don't be sorry that you lose a friend; I have no regrets.

BASSANIO. I'm married to a wife, who is dear to me as life itself. But I'd give up life itself, my wife and all the world, if only I could save you.

PORTIA. 'Your wife would give you little thanks for that, if she were by to hear you make the offer.'

SHYLOCK. We're wasting time. Please, declare your judgement.

PORTIA. A pound of that same merchant's flesh is yours.

SHYLOCK. A true judge!

PORTIA. Wait, Shylock! In this agreement, there's no mention of blood. You can take your pound of flesh; but if Antonio bleeds when you cut, then all your lands and possessions will be taken from you, according to the laws of Venice.

GRATIANO. Oh true judge!

SHYLOCK. Is that the law?

PORTIA. Yes, sir.

SHYLOCK. In that case, I accept the offer, and the merchant is free.

BASSANIO. Here is the money.

PORTIA. Wait! The moneylender can have only a pound of flesh as written in the agreement. So Shylock, carry on; remember a pound, no more, no less; and no blood please, otherwise you'll lose everything for breaking the laws of Venice.

SHYLOCK. I'll stay no longer.

PORTIA. Wait again, Shylock! By law, your wealth belongs to the state, because you planned to kill a citizen of Venice. Your life now depends on the decision of the Governor. Therefore, down on your knees, and ask him to forgive you.

GOVERNOR. So you'll understand what it means to forgive, I'll give you your life, even before you ask me. Then, I declare that half your wealth will go to Antonio, and the other half to the state.

PORTIA. What do you say, Antonio?

ANTONIO. I'll give up my part of his wealth, as long as Shylock agrees to leave this money to his daughter, when he dies. She's recently married a young man who's a dear friend of mine, and who is hated by Shylock.

PORTIA. Shylock, will you sign such an agreement?

SHYLOCK. Yes, I will. Please, let me go home now; I'm ill. Prepare the document, and send it to me to sign.

GOVERNOR. Go then, but remember to keep your promise.

[*Exit Shylock.*]

GOVERNOR [*to Portia*]. Sir, please come to my home for dinner.

PORTIA. I thank you, but I must be in Padua this night and will leave now.

GOVERNOR. As you wish. Antonio, I leave you to thank this gentleman, for he has saved your life.

[*Exit Governor.*]

BASSANIO. Sir, I and my friend have, by your wisdom, been saved this day. For this, we offer you the three thousand gold coins which were not paid to Shylock.

ANTONIO. And, forever, we'll be at your service.

PORTIA. I'm satisfied with the result, so need no other payment. I wish you well and now must leave you.

BASSANIO. Sir, I must insist that you take something from us, not as payment then, but to remember us by.

PORTIA. If you must insist, so be it. Give me your gloves, Bassanio; I'll wear them to remember you.

BASSANIO [*taking off his gloves*]. Here you are, sir.

PORTIA. 'And, for your love, I'll take this ring from you.' Do not pull back your hand, Bassanio; I ask for no more, just the ring.

BASSANIO. This ring, good sir? I'm sorry, but I cannot give it to you.

PORTIA. I want nothing but this ring.

BASSANIO. I'll buy you the most expensive ring in Venice, but I cannot give you this one.

PORTIA. First you offer, then you make me beg.

BASSANIO. Good sir, this ring was given to me by my wife; and when she put it on my finger, she made me promise never to sell it, lose it or give it to anyone.

PORTIA. That excuse is used by many men to save their gifts. You offend me. Come, Nerissa!

[*Exit Portia and Nerissa.*]

ANTONIO. Bassanio, let him have the ring. Surely your love for me, and what the man deserves, is stronger than your wife's command.

BASSANIO. You're right. Gratiano, run and give him the ring.

[*Exit Gratiano.*]

BASSANIO. Come, Antonio. In the morning early we'll go to Belmont.

[*Exit all.*]

Act 4 Scene 2

A street in Venice.

[*Enter Portia and Nerissa, still dressed as men.*]

PORTIA. Take this document to Shylock's house and get him to sign it. We'll leave tonight, and be home a day before our husbands. Shylock's daughter will be pleased with this agreement.

[*Enter Gratiano.*]

GRATIANO. Sir, my lord, Bassanio has taken good advice and sends this ring to you; he also wishes your company at dinner.

PORTIA. Dinner is impossible, but his ring I accept. Please thank him; also could you please show my assistant Shylock's house.

GRATIANO. Yes, madam.

NERISSA [*aside to Portia*]. I'll try and get my husband's ring, which he promised he would keep forever.

PORTIA [*aside to Nerissa*]. Yes, do so! Then we can have fun with them and pretend to be angry. Go now, and meet me later.

NERISSA. Come, good sir, will you show me Shylock's house?

[*Exit all.*]

Act 5 Scene 1

Belmont. Night. On the path up to Portia's house.

[*Enter Portia and Nerissa, dressed in their normal clothes.*]

PORTIA. See the light shining like a good action in a bad world.

NERISSA. Someone is coming.

[*Enter servant holding candle.*]

SERVANT. Welcome home, madam. I've come to lead the way.

PORTIA. We thank you. Have our husbands already returned?

SERVANT. Not yet.

PORTIA. Good! Go and tell the other servants we've arrived.

SERVANT. Yes, madam. But I think I hear your husband's trumpet.

[*Sound of trumpet.*]

[*Enter Bassanio, Antonio and Gratiano.*]

PORTIA. Welcome home, my lord, my husband.

BASSANIO. I thank you, madam. Give welcome to my friend, Antonio.

PORTIA. Sir, you're very welcome to our house.

GRATIANO [*to Nerissa*]. I gave it to the lawyer's assistant; don't be angry with me.

PORTIA. Oh, a quarrel already! What's the matter?

GRATIANO. All for a ring she gave me.

NERISSA. You promised you'd wear it till you died. You said these things, not I. Then you gave it to a lawyer's assistant! Might this assistant be another woman?

GRATIANO. No, sweet Nerissa!

PORTIA. I'm sorry Gratiano; but you're to blame. This was your wife's first gift to you. I gave Bassanio a ring too, and he promised never to take it off. If Bassanio ever did what you've done to Nerissa, I'd never forgive him.

BASSANIO [*aside*]. 'Why, I were best to cut my left hand off, and swear I lost the ring defending it.'

GRATIANO. My Lord Bassanio gave his ring to the lawyer; he really deserved it. Then the lawyer's assistant asked me for mine, and wouldn't take no for an answer.

PORTIA. What ring did you give to the lawyer, my lord? Not, I hope, the one you received from me.

BASSANIO. I can't deny it; you can see my finger; the ring has gone.

PORTIA. False heart! Forget me, until you can show me the ring once more.

NERISSA. And the same goes for you, Gratiano.

BASSANIO. Sweet Portia, if you understood why I had to give the ring away, you wouldn't be so angry.

PORTIA. If only you had thought for a moment about who gave you that ring, and what it meant, then you'd never have given it away. I'm beginning to suspect like Nerissa, that another woman has the ring.

BASSANIO. No, on my honour, madam, no woman has it. What should I say sweet lady? I was forced to give it to the lawyer, after he had saved my dear friend, Antonio's life. I'm sure, if you had been there, you too would have felt so grateful that you would have begged me to do so.

ANTONIO. I'm the unhappy subject of these quarrels.

PORTIA. Sir, do not worry; you're still welcome.

ANTONIO. I agreed to pay with my own life for Bassanio's wealth. And I'd have died, if it hadn't been for the wisdom of he who has your ring. I'll ensure that your Bassanio never breaks his promise to you again.

PORTIA. If you're responsible for his good word, then give him this ring, and tell him to keep it better than the first one.

ANTONIO. Here, Lord Bassanio.

BASSANIO. But, it's the same ring I gave the lawyer!

NERISSA. And here's a ring for you too, Gratiano.

GRATIANO. But, this too is the same one I gave the assistant. What can all this mean?

PORTIA. You're all amazed! Here's a letter from Bellario. If you read it, you'll see that Portia was the lawyer and Nerissa was her assistant. We too, have just arrived. Antonio, I also have a letter for you with better news than you can ever imagine. Your three ships have suddenly arrived in the harbour.

ANTONIO. I'm lost for words, like Bassanio and Gratiano. Sweet lady, you have not only given me life, but news of my good fortune too!

PORTIA. It's almost morning, but I'm sure that you're all still not satisfied. So, let's go in, and you can question us about these events.

BASSANIO. Yes, my love.

GRATIANO. And, 'while I live I'll fear no other thing so sore as keeping safe Nerissa's ring'.

[*Exit all.*]

Stop & Check

1 **Choose the best answer – A, B or C, about *The Merchant of Venice*.**

1 Antonio
   A ☐ borrows money from his friends.
   B ☐ helps people in need.
   C ☐ does the same job as Shylock.

2 Portia's house is in
   A ☐ Padua.
   B ☐ Venice.
   C ☐ Belmont.

3 Nerissa falls in love with
   A ☐ Antonio.
   B ☐ Gratiano.
   C ☐ Bassanio.

4 Portia writes to her cousin Bellario
   A ☐ for advice about Antonio.
   B ☐ to invite him to her wedding.
   C ☐ to complain about Bassanio.

5 Shylock cannot have his pound of flesh because
   A ☐ there isn't a surgeon.
   B ☐ there must be no blood.
   C ☐ his knife isn't sharp enough.

6 In the end, Shylock
   A ☐ is sent to prison.
   B ☐ is forgiven by the governor.
   C ☐ takes the money.

7 In the end, Shylock agrees to
   A ☐ buy Antonio three new ships.
   B ☐ leave money to his daughter when he dies.
   C ☐ leave Venice.

Writing

2 **Read the following quote from *The Merchant of Venice* and answer the questions.**

'This house, these servants, and this same myself are yours, my lord. I give them with this ring.'

1 Who is Portia speaking to and on what occasion?
2 Why is the ring important to the story?

Vocabulary

3 **Complete the sentences with a verb from the box in the correct form. The verb may be affirmative or negative.**

insult • beg • spoil • trust • deserve • lack • deny

1 Bassanio _____ Portia to forgive him for breaking his promise, but she refused.

2 Shylock hates Antonio, because the kind merchant _____ his lending business.

3 Bassanio could not _____ that he no longer had Portia's ring.

4 Antonio _____ _____ to die, because he was a good man.

5 Bassanio _____ the means to dress elegantly, because he had spent all his money.

6 Antonio _____ _____ Shylock many times in the past, but now he needed him.

7 Bassanio _____ _____ Shylock, and didn't want Antonio to sign the agreement.

PRE-READING ACTIVITY

Grammar for First

4 **Read about the next play, *The Tempest*. Complete the text with one word for each gap.**

One of the (**1**)_____ interesting aspects of *The Tempest* is the use of magic, which can have (**2**)_____ good and bad consequences. Prospero, (**3**)_____ lives on a strange island with his daughter Miranda, uses his magic powers (**4**)_____ create a storm and bring his brother Antonio to the island. Years before, his brother (**5**)_____ sent him away from Milan so he could become duke. Now Prospero wants to punish his brother and get his position (**6**)_____. There's a love story in this play as (**7**)_____. The King of Naples' son, Ferdinand, meets Miranda on the island and (**8**)_____ in love with her. However, he'll have to prove he deserves Miranda, before (**9**)_____ accepted into the family by Prospero.

The Tempest[1]

Characters:

PROSPERO, *the true Duke of Milan.*

MIRANDA, *Prospero's daughter.*

ARIEL, *a spirit and Prospero's servant.*

CALIBAN, *a monster, son of the witch, Sycorax.*

ANTONIO, *Prospero's brother.*

ALONSO, *King of Naples.*

FERDINAND, *Alonso's son.*

GONZALO, *a kind lord.*

Prospero, an old man, lives with his daughter, Miranda, on an island. Their home is a cave. A spirit called Ariel, and a monster called Caliban, are Prospero's servants. Prospero is very interested in magic and has learnt a lot about it from his books over the past twelve years. One night, with the help of Ariel, he creates a violent storm. There's a ship at sea which has been badly damaged by the tempest, and is about to sink.

Act 1 Scene 1

The Island. On the shore. Thunder, lightning, rain, high waves.

[Enter Prospero and Miranda. They look towards the sea.]

1. **tempest:** 暴風雨

MIRANDA. If you've made this storm, father, then please stop it; I fear that some creatures may be harmed by its power. Look! There's a ship in trouble! Can you do nothing to help those on board?

PROSPERO. Don't worry, my dear daughter. 'There's no harm done.' I've organised it, so that everybody on the ship will be saved. I've done all this for you, Miranda. You don't know anything about your past. All you know of me, is that I'm your father who lives in a poor cave. Can you remember anything before coming to this island? Probably not; you were only three years old.

MIRANDA. Certainly, sir, I can.

PROSPERO. What? Please, tell me, my child, what can you remember?

MIRANDA. It seems more like a dream and so long ago; but didn't I have four or five women who looked after me?

PROSPERO. Yes, you did, and more, Miranda. Can you also remember how you got here?

MIRANDA. No, I'm afraid not.

PROSPERO. Twelve years ago, I, your father, was Duke of Milan; you were my only child and treated like a princess.

MIRANDA. What happened to bring us to this island?

PROSPERO. Well, I wanted to concentrate on studying art, magic and other subjects, so I left my duties as Duke of Milan to my younger brother, Antonio.

MIRANDA. You mean I have an uncle?

PROSPERO. Yes, my dear child; but he proved to be unworthy of my trust. Once he had the power of duke, Antonio became ambitious, and feared that, one day, I might want my position back. With the help of the King of Naples, who was my enemy at that time, he planned to kill us.

MIRANDA. And how did we manage to escape such a cruel fate?

PROSPERO. Since my people loved me so much, he had to make our murder seem an accident. Antonio took us on a ship, and when we were far out at sea, he forced us into a smaller boat and left us there to die.

MIRANDA. So, how were we saved?

PROSPERO. A kind lord, Gonzalo, had secretly put food and water in the boat, so we managed to survive. He even remembered some of my books.

MIRANDA. Oh! My poor father! Was I much trouble?

PROSPERO. Not at all; you were a little angel and your smiles kept me cheerful. Our food lasted until we reached this island where we've been ever since.

MIRANDA. I thank you, father, for everything you've done for me; but why did you start the storm?

PROSPERO. I did it for revenge. My enemies, the King of Naples, and my cruel brother Antonio, are on that ship out there. Because of this storm, they'll be forced to abandon their sinking ship, and will come to this island in search of safety. Meanwhile, sleep my child, until they arrive.

[*Exit all.*]

Act 1 Scene 2

A wood on the island.

[*Enter Prospero and the spirit, Ariel.*]

PROSPERO. Well, my brave spirit, how did you do your business?

ARIEL. As you commanded, my lord. There was thunder and lightning and waves higher than the ship itself!

PROSPERO. Did anyone stay calm?

ARIEL. No, not one. They were all desperate. Ferdinand, the king's son, was the first to abandon the ship and dive into the dark waters of the sea. Then, all the others followed.

PROSPERO. That's my spirit! But, they were near the shore, weren't they?

ARIEL. Yes, they're all safe, but I made them land on different parts of the island. Ferdinand is well, and not even his clothes have been ruined by the sea-water; he's just sad, because he wrongly thinks his father, the king, has drowned.

PROSPERO. Wonderful, Ariel! Bring him here; I want my daughter, Miranda, to meet this young prince. What about the king and my brother?

ARIEL. They are desperately looking for Ferdinand. As for the rest of the sailors, all of them reached the shore safely. Even the ship is safe in the harbour, but it's invisible to them.

PROSPERO. Ariel, you've done a good job; but there's still more work to do.

ARIEL. More work? But, master, you promised me my freedom. I've done everything you asked well, without complaining.

PROSPERO. What's this talk, Ariel? Don't you remember when I released you from the tree, which had become your prison, because of an evil witch? What was her name again?

ARIEL. Sycorax, sir.

PROSPERO. Ah, yes, now I remember. She was left on this island by sailors due to her evil actions. Then, when you refused to carry out her terrible orders, she shut you up inside a tree for twelve years. In the meantime, Sycorax died, and her monster of a son, Caliban ruled the island. You were left trapped in the tree until I found you. Do you remember now?

ARIEL. Yes, my lord. And now, Caliban is your servant, and I enjoy annoying him. I beg you to forgive me, my lord. I didn't wish to seem ungrateful. I'll do whatever you ask of me.

PROSPERO. Good! Go and fetch me Ferdinand.

ARIEL. Yes, sir.

PROSPERO. And I'll go and wake Miranda, so she can meet the prince.

Act 1 Scene 3

A wood on the island, where Caliban lives. While looking for Ferdinand, Ariel sees Caliban.

[*Enter Caliban, followed by Ariel. Caliban can't see Ariel, but he can hear him.*]

ARIEL [*aside*]. There's Caliban! I'll play some tricks on this nasty, lazy monster.

[*Ariel pushes Caliban from behind.*]

CALIBAN. Is that you Ariel? Stop annoying me! I'm tired.

ARIEL. Do your work, you lazy monster! Instead of being grateful to Prospero, who taught you to speak, you were unkind to his sweet daughter, Miranda, and were sent away from Prospero's cave to live in this dark, dirty place.

CALIBAN. I don't care. I hate Prospero, and his daughter, and you! This island should only be mine.

[*Ariel becomes a snake and bites Caliban's toe.*]

CALIBAN. Ow! That hurt! I'm getting out of here! [*running away.*]

ARIEL. Don't worry; I have more important business to do.

[*Exit all.*]

Act 1 Scene 4

In front of Prospero's cave.

[*Enter Prospero and Miranda. They sit down under a big tree.*]

MIRANDA. Father, have I slept long?

PROSPERO. You've slept enough. Let's talk a little. The fire needs more wood. Where is that lazy Caliban?

MIRANDA. I don't know or care. I can't stand him.

PROSPERO. I know, my dear; he's unkind. I'd have taught Caliban more, but he has the same evil nature as his mother, the witch, Sycorax. This stops him from learning anything more useful. But, hush my dear; who's that creature coming this way. Let's stay here and watch.

[*Enter Ariel, followed by Ferdinand.*]

[*Ariel is invisible to all, except Prospero. Although Ferdinand can't see the spirit, he can hear Ariel singing, and has followed the sound.*]

FERDINAND. Where's this music coming from? It must be the music of some god of this island. While I was crying for my dear drowned father, this song came across the waters and calmed the angry waves and my grief with its sweet sound, so I followed it. [*looking up at the sky.*]

PROSPERO. Miranda, what can you see, my child? Apart from me, your father, you've never seen any other human being.

MIRANDA. Oh father! It's a beautiful creature; what is it? Is it a spirit? Look how it looks about!

PROSPERO. No, my child; it eats and sleeps just like us. This is a young man; he was on the ship that sank in the storm. He'd be handsome if it weren't for the sad expression on his face.

You see, my dear daughter, he has lost his travelling companions, and is wandering about, looking for them.

MIRANDA. My father, I've never seen such natural beauty in a man!

PROSPERO [*aside*]. Well done Ariel; everything's going as planned.

[*Ferdinand sees Miranda and is struck by her beauty.*]

FERDINAND. The wonder of your beauty assures me that you must be the goddess of this magical island. Please, stay here with me and give me some good advice.

MIRANDA. I'm no goddess, just a girl.

FERDINAND. Oh joy! This sweet lady speaks my language!

PROSPERO [*aside*]. Delicate Ariel, it's love at first sight! You'll soon have the freedom you deserve. However, before I give him my daughter's heart, I must see if Ferdinand has courage and if he's loyal. [*to Ferdinand, angrily.*] I fear you have come here with the idea of taking this island from me, young man!

MIRANDA [*aside*]. Why does my father speak so unkindly? This is the first man I've ever sighed for.

FERDINAND. I assure you, my lord, I haven't come to take your island.

MIRANDA. Can you not see, dear father, that he's full of kindness?

PROSPERO [*to Ferdinand*]. Follow me – [*to Miranda*]. Don't speak for him; he has come to trick us.

[*to Ferdinand*]. Come, I'll tie your feet to your neck and make you drink sea-water.

FERDINAND. No! A more powerful enemy is needed to make me do such things.

[*Ferdinand pulls out his sword, but Prospero touches the young man's shoulder, and suddenly Ferdinand can no longer move.*]

MIRANDA. Please father, don't be too hard on him, for he is kind and gentle.

PROSPERO. Silence! One word more, Miranda, and I'll become angry with you too. How can you judge this man when you know no others to compare him with? I assure you, there are many more much better than him.

MIRANDA. I've no ambition to see a better man; he's more than enough for my affections.

PROSPERO [*to Ferdinand*]. Come! You're forced to obey me, as I've taken power over your movements. Follow me to my cave.

FERDINAND. How strange, I can't stop myself following you; but my weakness, the loss of my father and all my companions, is nothing compared to the thought of never seeing this beautiful lady again. I'll suffer anything as long as I see my sweet lady once more.

MIRANDA. Do not fear, my father has a better nature than what it seems.

PROSPERO. Miranda, silence! Come, young man.

[*Exit All.*]

Act 2 Scene 1

In front of Prospero's cave.

[Enter Ferdinand, carrying a heavy piece of wood for the fire.]

FERDINAND. This work is hard and I hate it, but the lady I must serve makes it pass quickly. She's ten times more gentle than her father, who has given me this job of fetching thousands of pieces of heavy wood. I see my sweet lady's tears as she watches my pain, and I feel strong again.

[Enter Miranda, followed by Prospero who hides, so that the two young lovers cannot see him.]

MIRANDA. Please, don't work so hard! Come and sit down and rest. My father is busy studying and won't notice.

[Ferdinand sits down next to Miranda.]

FERDINAND. Oh most dear mistress! The sun will have set before I manage to finish.

MIRANDA. I'll help you; give me some wood to carry.

FERDINAND. No, my sweet lady; I'd rather break my back than have you work for me. But, tell me, what's your name?

MIRANDA. Miranda – Oh! I forgot; my father told me not to tell you.

[Prospero smiles at his daughter's words.]

FERDINAND. Oh Miranda! I've seen many beautiful women in my life, but you're the most perfect!

MIRANDA. I don't know any other women; only my own face in the mirror. As for men, I've only ever seen you, my dear friend, and my father. I don't know what other men abroad look like, but 'I would not wish any companion in the world but you'. Oh dear! I'm speaking too much and forgetting my father's advice.

FERDINAND. I'm a prince, Miranda. My name's Ferdinand. Actually, I'm probably now King of Naples, even if I wish it were not so. You'll be my queen! 'The very instant that I saw you did my heart fly to your service.'

MIRANDA. Do you love me?

FERDINAND. Oh heaven! [*on his knees.*] I love you more than anything else in the world!

MIRANDA. I'm so happy, I could cry!

PROSPERO [*aside*]. How sweet their love is!

MIRANDA. I'm your wife, if you'll marry me.

FERDINAND. My mistress, dearest!

MIRANDA. My husband then?

FERDINAND. Yes, with a willing heart

MIRANDA. And mine too is more than willing.

[*Prospero comes out from his hiding place.*]

PROSPERO. Ferdinand, if your punishment has been too hard, you can now enjoy your reward. I happily give you my daughter's hand.

MIRANDA. Oh father!

PROSPERO. Worry no more, my child. I've heard the words of love you have exchanged and fully approve of your plans to marry. Ferdinand, I wished only to see if you truly loved my beautiful, sweet, daughter.

FERDINAND. I do.

PROSPERO. Then, go and talk some more. I have other business to attend to.

MIRANDA. Thank you, my father! [*to Ferdinand.*] Come, my love, and tell me of your life.

[*Exit Miranda and Ferdinand, holding hands.*]

PROSPERO. I wonder what the others are doing. I must go and look for Ariel.

[*Exit Prospero.*]

Act 3 Scene 1
Another part of the island.
[*Enter Antonio, Alonso and Gonzalo.*]

GONZALO. Sir, I can go no further; my old bones are aching. I need to rest.

ALONSO. Old lord, I can't blame you. I too am tired. I fear we'll never find my son, Ferdinand.

ANTONIO. I can't go on either. But, listen to this strange song! What can it mean? Look!

[*Enter Ariel, singing. He is dressed as a servant. He brings a table full of food and drink.*]

[*Exit Ariel.*]

GONZALO. Wonderful, sweet music! And look at all this food! Won't you try some?

ANTONIO. Not I; it could be poisonous.

ALONSO. I'll try; the worst has already happened to me. Come sirs, eat with me.

[*Thunder and lightning. Enter Ariel again. He now seems an enormous, terrifying bird.*]

ARIEL. Antonio! Alonso! You are two evil men. Well may you tremble at my sight, for I've come to remind you of your terrible crime against Prospero. I'll make you go mad with guilt.

ANTONIO. We'll fight you with our swords! [*taking out sword.*]

ARIEL. Put away your sword; it's useless against me. I'm like the force of nature that brought you to this island. Antonio, do you remember how you became Duke of Milan? Then, you made Prospero suffer the dangers of the sea; not only him, but also his innocent child.

That same sea has now shown its anger for your crime and thrown you onto this island. Alonso, you've lost your son. Now you must show your regret for all the evil actions you've done in the past. You and your companions must pay for your crimes!

[*Thunder; Ariel leaves taking the food and drink with him.*]

GONZALO. My lord, what was that?

ALONSO. Oh it's a terrifying monster, I thought I saw; and it seemed to speak to me; and the thunder shouted Prospero's name. Now I remember how cruel I've been. Poor Prospero! His poor sweet daughter, lost at sea because of our actions, Antonio.

ANTONIO. You're right, my lord; and I'm to blame even more than you, because I betrayed my own brother, my own blood, and my sweet, innocent niece. Let's go and look for the monster. Maybe he can tell us what happened to my brother.

[*Exit Antonio and Alonso.*]

GONZALO. They're both desperate. I think guilt has entered like poison into their blood. I must go after them and try to help them. How wonderful it would be if Prospero were still alive!

[*Exit Gonzalo.*]

Act 4 Scene 1

Outside Prospero's cave.

[*Enter Prospero and Ariel.*]

PROSPERO. Come and tell me what you've been doing.

ARIEL. Reminding your enemies of their cruel actions. They were already going mad with hunger and thirst. Now their guilt has made them even worse.

PROSPERO. Do they really regret all the terrible things they've done?

ARIEL. Yes, my lord; I'm sure of this. I saw their despair with my own eyes and felt pity for them.

PROSPERO. If you, who are a spirit can feel pity, then I, as a human being should feel the same. It's time for you to bring them to me, so that I can forgive them.

ARIEL. I'll fetch them, sir.

[*Exit Ariel.*]

PROSPERO. Now, I'll rest until Ariel returns.

[*Exit Prospero.*]

Act 5 Scene 1

Outside Prospero's cave. Entrance to cave covered by a curtain.

[Enter Prospero. He draws a circle on the ground.]

PROSPERO. I can hear Ariel coming with my brother and the others. I'll make them stand in this magic circle, until I'm sure that they regret all they've done.

[Enter Ariel, followed by Alonso, Antonio and Gonzalo. Ariel leads them into the circle, where they stand as Prospero observes them. All three are so frightened, that they don't recognise Prospero.]

PROSPERO. Before I speak to these humans, Ariel, I give you your freedom as promised. I'll miss you.

ARIEL. Thank you, my lord.

PROSPERO. One last thing; in the harbour, you'll find the ship with all the sailors asleep on board. Go and wake them up and tell them to prepare the ship to go home.

ARIEL. I will, my sir; and before I leave you forever, I'll direct the wind to take you safely back to Milan.

[Exit Ariel.]

PROSPERO. Now, I must free these terrified minds from their despair.

[Prospero waves his hands in the air. The circle disappears and the three men are no longer frightened. They still don't recognise Prospero.]

PROSPERO. First you, good Gonzalo! Your actions saved my life and that of my sweet daughter. I'll make sure everyone knows of your kindness.

GONZALO. I fear I don't know you, my lord.

PROSPERO. Gonzalo, I'm Prospero, the real Duke of Milan, who you so kindly helped all those years ago.

GONZALO. Oh, my lord, I thought I'd never see you again!

PROSPERO. Welcome, also to my lord Alonso, King of Naples. You too were part of my brother Antonio's evil plan, but I forgive you.

ALONSO. Whether you be Prospero or not, I'm not sure. All I

know is that, since I saw you, the madness in my mind has gone.

PROSPERO. And finally, Antonio! You don't deserve to be called my brother anymore. Despite your evil plan, I've survived all these years. Now, I demand that the position of Duke of Milan be mine again.

ANTONIO. I beg you to forgive me my brother, and promise that, from now on, you'll be known once more as Duke of Milan.

ALONSO. But, please tell us; how did you find us? We've been all over the island, searching for my lost son.

PROSPERO. I'm sorry for your loss, sir.

ALONSO. I can no longer hope to find my dear Ferdinand. He's been missing for too long.

PROSPERO. I too have lost a child; a daughter.

ALONSO. You? Your daughter? I wish they were both living in Naples where they'd become king and queen. When did you lose your daughter?

PROSPERO. In this last tempest. Anyway, be assured that I'm indeed Prospero, Duke of Milan. Thanks to Gonzalo, I survived and came to this island, where I have lived all these years. I do not have much, just this cave. Why not come and rest in it for a while, my lord? I'm sure you will find great pleasure in seeing what there is inside.

[*Prospero pulls open the curtain at the entrance to the cave, and Alonso sees Ferdinand and Miranda sitting there playing chess.*]

ALONSO. If this is another vision of this island, then I've lost my son again!

FERDINAND. Father! The sea has been kind to you; you're safe! [*hugging his father.*]

MIRANDA: How many handsome creatures there are here!

ALONSO. Who is this beautiful creature Ferdinand? Is she the goddess of this island?

FERDINAND. No, dear father; I thought the same when I first saw her. She's human like us, only of extraordinary beauty. I've chosen her to be my wife. She's Miranda, the daughter of this man, Prospero, Duke of Milan. He's been like a father to me.

ALONSO. And I'll be like a father to Miranda. How awful that I must start by asking my daughter to forgive me.

PROSPERO. No sir, There's no need. All that is now in the past. Even you, Antonio, no longer need to feel sorry. By sending us to this island, Miranda has met Ferdinand, and will one day become Queen of Naples!

ANTONIO. Oh, my dear brother! Thank you for your kind words. [*hugging Prospero.*]

GONZALO. How wonderful! Ferdinand has found a wife; Alonso has found his son; and Prospero will be Duke of Milan once more!

ALONSO. Ferdinand and Miranda, I wish you every happiness. But how can we return home?

PROSPERO. Do not fear, my lord. Your ship and all you sailors are safe in the harbour, waiting for us.

ALONSO. These aren't natural events, but it doesn't matter. It's enough to know that we can all return home safely.

PROSPERO. Tonight you'll be my guests, before starting our journey home tomorrow. I'll entertain you with the story of my life here on the island. Then, in the morning, we'll leave for Naples, where our two dear children will be married. Then, to Milan, where I'll live the rest of my days.

[*Exit all except Prospero.*]

[*Prospero takes his books about magic and buries them in the ground.*]

PROSPERO. I now have everything I've ever dreamt of. My sweet daughter has found love and will become Queen of Naples, and I'll be Duke of Milan once more. No more magic; no more spirits; I've forgiven all and no longer need them. I'm the happiest man in the world.

Stop & Check

1 **Are the following statements about *The Tempest* true (T) or false (F)? Correct the false ones.**

	T	F
1 Prospero used to be King of Naples before living on the island.	☐	☐
2 Miranda has been on the island for the past three years.	☐	☐
3 Caliban, the monster, used to rule the island before Prospero arrived.	☐	☐
4 Caliban, the monster, appears to Antonio, Alonso and Gonzalo and frightens them.	☐	☐
5 Prospero decides to forgive his brother and Alonso because Ariel asks him to do so.	☐	☐
6 Prospero puts his brother, Alonso and Gonzalo in a magic circle.	☐	☐
7 Prospero gives his books on magic to Caliban at the end of the play.	☐	☐

Grammar

2 **Complete the sentences with the right alternative.**

1 Prospero was very *interested/keen* on magic and read many books on the subject.

2 In Milan, Miranda used to have several servants who *cared/looked* after her.

3 Ariel *got/made* Alonso and Ferdinand land on different parts of the island.

4 Sycorax was left on the island *due/because* of her evil actions.

5 Miranda had never seen any other man *apart/besides* from her father.

6 Prospero *agreed/approved* of Miranda's plan to marry Ferdinand.

7 Prospero was *blamed/betrayed* by his brother and left to die on a small boat.

Speaking / Writing

3a **Discuss with a partner the character of Miranda in _The Tempest_. Consider the following:**

- Her relationship with her father, Prospero.
- How her character changes during the play.
- Her relationship with Ferdinand.

3b **Now write a summary about Miranda's character. Give reasons for what you like or don't like about her.**

_____

_____

_____

_____

_____

_____

_____

_____

PRE-READING ACTIVITY

Listening

4 **The next play, _Twelfth Night_, is a romantic comedy. This time twins, Sebastian and Viola, are so alike that they cause a lot of confusion. Listen to the conversation between the Captain and Viola in Act 1 Scene 1. Imagine what will happen next. Answer the following questions, then check at the end of the play to see if you were right.**

1 Will Viola get the job with Orsino? Why/why not?

2 Will Sebastian become Orsino's new servant instead of Viola? Why/ why not?

3 Will Olivia agree to see Orsino? Why/ why not?

4 Will Olivia answer Orsino's letters? Why/ why not?

5 Will Orsino marry Olivia? Why/ why not?

6 Will Sebastian tell Olivia that Cesario is really his sister Viola? Why/why not?

Twelfth Night, or What You Will

Characters:

ORSINO,	*Governor of Illyria.*
SEBASTIAN,	*Viola's twin brother.*
ANTONIO,	*a sea captain and Sebastian's friend.*
OLIVIA,	*a rich lady.*
VIOLA / CESARIO,	*Sebastian's twin sister.*
CAPTAIN OF SHIP,	Viola's friend.
A GENTLEMAN,	*in love with Olivia.*
A PRIEST.	
TWO OFFICERS.	
OLIVIA'S SERVANT.	

Viola, a young lady from Messaline, and her identical[1] twin brother Sebastian, decide to travel across the seas. One night, there's a violent storm; their ship hits a rock and starts to sink off the coast of Illyria. The captain of the ship manages to reach land safely with Viola, but there's no sign of Sebastian.

Act 1 Scene 1

The sea coast.

[Enter Viola and Captain.]

VIOLA. What country is this?

---

1. identical: 一模一樣

CAPTAIN. Illyria.

VIOLA. And what will I do in Illyria without my dear brother, Sebastian? Do you think he has drowned?

CAPTAIN. The last time I saw your brother, madam, he was floating on a large piece of wood, rising above the waves; so perhaps he has survived.

VIOLA. Oh, how I hope so! But, tell me sir, do you know this country?

CAPTAIN. Yes, madam; I was born and grew up near here.

VIOLA. Who governs here?

CAPTAIN. A kind man called Orsino.

VIOLA. Orsino! I used to hear my father talk about him; Orsino wasn't married then.

CAPTAIN. He's still single, but in love with a beautiful, rich lady called Olivia.

VIOLA. What do you know of her?

CAPTAIN. The sad lady lost her father a year ago; but worse still, her dear and only brother then died too, leaving her all alone. Since her brother's death, she refuses all company.

VIOLA. Oh how I wish I could help this lady, who suffers for her lost brother, just like me.

CAPTAIN. She won't even see the governor, who sends her messages of love every day.

VIOLA. You're a kind man, captain. Please help me to become Orsino's messenger[1]. In this way, I'll take his love letters to Olivia and become her friend.

CAPTAIN. But you can't; you're a girl.

VIOLA. This is where I need you. You'll help me dress as a boy, so that Orsino will take me as his messenger.

CAPTAIN. If this plan makes you happy, then I'll help you for sure, madam, and it'll be our secret.

VIOLA. Thank you. Let's go now and prepare this disguise. Then,

---

1. **messenger:** 信差

you can introduce me to Orsino as an excellent servant.

CAPTAIN. With boy's clothes, you'll surely look like your brother Sebastian; you're identical. But, what will you call yourself?

VIOLA. I'll be known as Cesario.

CAPTAIN. Excellent! So be it!

[*Exit all.*]

Act 1 Scene 2

A room in Orsino's Palace.

[*Enter Viola, dressed as the boy servant, Cesario.*]

VIOLA. I've only known Orsino for a few days, but already he has opened his heart to me; how lucky Olivia is to have this man's love. I'd certainly not refuse his favours. Hush! Here he comes!

[*Enter Orsino.*]

ORSINO. Cesario!

VIOLA. Here I am, my lord.

ORSINO. My dear, trusted Cesario, you must help me capture sweet Olivia's broken heart. Go to the lady's home and don't leave until she opens her door to you.

VIOLA. But, my lord, there's such sadness in her heart that she'll surely refuse to let me in.

ORSINO. You must succeed, Cesario.

VIOLA. And if I manage to speak to her, my lord, what then?

ORSINO. Then, tell her of the passion of my love; your young delicate features and sweet voice are ideal. Believe me, my boy, you have the kind nature of a woman, which makes you perfect for this affair.

VIOLA. I think not, my lord.

ORSINO. If you succeed, I promise you freedom and wealth.

VIOLA. I'll do my best, to win your lady's love: [*aside.*] but, I must fight against my own feelings! For I'd happily be the wife of this man whose love I must declare to another woman.

[*Exit all.*]

Act 1 Scene 3

A room in Olivia's house.

[*Enter Olivia and servant.*]

SERVANT. Madam, there's a young gentleman at the gate who wishes to speak to you.

OLIVIA. From the governor Orsino?

SERVANT. I know only that he's a handsome young man, madam, and speaks very well. He's determined to see you.

OLIVIA. Then, let him in; but I'll turn my back on him.

SERVANT. I'll fetch him now, madam.

[*Exit servant.*]

[*Enter Viola.*]

VIOLA. Are you the lady of the house?

OLIVIA. Speak to me.

VIOLA. Your beauty has no match; but, please tell me; are you the lady of the house, because I've never seen her.

OLIVIA. I am.

VIOLA. Then I can continue praising your beauty before coming to the heart of my message.

OLIVIA. Please, come to the point and forget the rest.

VIOLA. But, I'm a messenger.

OLIVIA. So, what's written in your message?

VIOLA [*reading*]. Most sweet lady,….

OLIVIA. Who's it from?

VIOLA. From Orsino's heart.

OLIVIA. Oh! I've heard it all before. Have you nothing else to say?

VIOLA. 'Good madam, let me see your face.'

OLIVIA. This request isn't part of your message, but I'll satisfy your curiosity. [*turns round.*]

Look, sir. Do you not think I am well-made?

VIOLA. 'Excellently done, if God did it all.'

OLIVIA. It is so, sir; it'll last over time.

VIOLA. Madam, you'd surely be the cruellest lady alive if you were to die without leaving the world with a copy of your beauty.

OLIVIA. Oh! sir, I won't be so hard-hearted. I'll make a list of my features; red lips, two grey eyes, one neck, one chin, and so on. Were you sent to praise me?

VIOLA. You're too proud; but my master loves you.

OLIVIA. How does he love me?

VIOLA. With adoration, with tears, with sighs of love and fire.

OLIVIA. Your lord knows my mind; I can't love him, even though he's young, rich and handsome.

VIOLA. If I loved you with my master's passion, I wouldn't accept no, for an answer.

OLIVIA. What would you do?

VIOLA. I'd stay at your gate and sing you songs of love all night long. Then, I'd call your name until you changed your mind.

OLIVIA. You'd do all of this for me? But, tell me, what are your origins?

VIOLA. I'm a gentleman.

OLIVIA. Go back to your lord. Tell him not to send you here anymore, unless, by chance, you decide to come and tell me his reaction to my words. Goodbye.

VIOLA. Goodbye, sweet cruelty.

[*Exit Viola.*]

OLIVIA. What a gentleman! Such a delicate face; such sweet words. If he were the master, I'd freely give him my heart.

[*Enter servant.*]

SERVANT. Madam, do you need me?

OLIVIA. Yes indeed! [*taking a ring from her finger.*] Run after that messenger boy, and give him this ring back. Tell him, his master must forget me.

SERVANT. Yes, madam.

[*Exit Servant.*]

OLIVIA. What's happening to me? If it's my fate to love this young messenger, then let it be so!

[*Exit Olivia.*]

Act 2 Scene 1

A street near Olivia's house.

[*Enter Viola, followed by Olivia's servant.*]

SERVANT. Weren't you with my lady Olivia just now?

VIOLA. Yes; Why?

SERVANT. She returns this ring to you, sir. Tell your master not to hope for her love.

[*Exit servant.*]

VIOLA. I left no ring with her. What does this lady mean? I hope she hasn't found me so charming as to fall in love with me! Heaven forbid! But, now I remember the love in her eyes as she spoke to me. And now, this ring; she knows I'll surely try to give it back to her. Poor lady! She'd be better loving a dream. My disguise causes such pain. How can all this be solved? She loves me; my master loves her; and poor me! I'm in love with my master!

[*Exit Viola.*]

Act 2 Scene 2

A room in Orsino's palace.

[*Enter Orsino and Viola.*]

ORSINO. Cesario, what did you think of the song we heard last night?

VIOLA. It clearly expressed the adoration and pains of love.

ORSINO. My boy, your words, and the sadness in your eyes, seem those of one who suffers for love, despite your youth. Isn't it so?

VIOLA. It could be, if it were to please you.

ORSINO. What kind of woman has stolen your heart?

VIOLA. A woman of your age and similar features.

ORSINO. Then, she's too old for you, my boy! Remember, it's always better to go for a younger woman.

VIOLA. I'll remember that, my lord; but the heart is commanded only by love.

ORSINO. So true, my boy! Look how desperate I am! Return to my cruel love and tell her that I'm not attracted by her wealth, but by the miracle of her beauty.

VIOLA. But if she can't love you, sir?

ORSINO. I can't accept this answer. No woman could ever love a man as much as I adore my sweet Olivia!

VIOLA. But, I know well, how much a woman can love a man. My father had a daughter who loved a man, as much as I'd love a man, were I a woman.

ORSINO. And what happened to her?

VIOLA. Nothing; she never told him of her love. 'She sat like Patience on a monument, smiling at grief.' Enough of this sad story; shall I go to your lady now, sir?

ORSINO. Yes, come, and I'll give you the letter for her.

[*Exit all.*]

Act 3 Scene 1

Olivia's Garden.

[*Enter Olivia and servant.*]

SERVANT. Madam, the gentleman from yesterday is here.

OLIVIA. Then, bring him to me!

[*Exit servant.*]

[*Enter Viola.*]

VIOLA. Most excellent lady!

OLIVIA. What's your name?

VIOLA. Cesario, my lady.

OLIVIA. Give me your hand, sir.

VIOLA. My duty, madam, is to be your servant.

OLIVIA. You're Orsino's servant.

VIOLA. And he is yours, and what belongs to him is yours.

OLIVIA. My thoughts aren't for him.

VIOLA. But, madam, I come to tell you of his thoughts for you.

OLIVIA. Please, never speak of him again; but if you wish to talk of something else, I'd rather hear your words than music from heaven.

VIOLA. Dear lady...

OLIVIA. Didn't I make my passion for you clear when I gave my servant the ring for you? I've shown you my heart. Now, let me hear you speak.

VIOLA. I pity[1] you.

OLIVIA. That's a kind of love.

VIOLA. No; very often we pity our enemies.

[*Clock strikes.*]

OLIVIA. The sound of the clock makes me realise how I've wasted my time.

VIOLA. Have you no message for my master, good lady?

OLIVIA. No; instead, please, tell me what you think of me.

VIOLA. That you aren't what you think you are.

OLIVIA. I think the same of you.

VIOLA. 'Then think you right: I am not what I am.'

OLIVIA. Cesario, I love you so much, that neither reason nor pride can hide my passion for you.

VIOLA. I promise you that no woman has my heart and never will. So, goodbye, good madam: I'll worry you no more with my master's

---

1. pity: 同情

tears.

OLIVIA. But come again; for perhaps, your heart which now hates me, may be moved by love.

[*Exit Viola.*]

OLIVIA. I can't stand to be without Cesario for even a minute. I'll send my servant to run after him and bring him back to me.

[*Exit Olivia.*]

Act 3 Scene 2

A street near Olivia's house.

[*Enter Viola, quickly followed by a gentleman.*]

GENTLEMAN. Sir, prepare to defend yourself!

VIOLA. You're making a mistake, sir. I have no quarrel with you.

GENTLEMAN. You've stolen my love, my joy.

VIOLA. Sir, are you in love with some woman? For if this is the case, I can assure you that no woman has captured my heart.

GENTLEMAN. I see your cruelty goes beyond all reason. You've stolen my sweet Olivia's heart with words borrowed from your master. You've succeeded in winning her heart, where I've failed; and now you dare make her suffer, by playing with her emotions. Therefore, I challenge you to fight with your sword, so I may save the honour of my sweet lady, and perhaps win back her heart. [*pulling out sword.*]

VIOLA [*aside*]. How can I defend myself? Perhaps the only way is to admit I'm not a man.

[*Enter Antonio, a sea captain and friend of Viola's identical twin brother, Sebastian.*]

ANTONIO. Put down your sword, sir. [*pointing to Viola.*] If this young gentleman has offended you, I'll fight you for him. [*pulling out his sword.*]

GENTLEMAN. You, sir! Why? Who are you?

ANTONIO. One who loves this boy dearly. I've already saved him once from drowning in a storm at sea. Now, I'm ready to save him again from the sharp point of your sword.

GENTLEMAN. Then, I accept your challenge; but look! Some officers are coming.

[*Enter two officers.*]

FIRST OFFICER [*pointing at Antonio*]. This is the man.

SECOND OFFICER. Antonio, I arrest you for a crime committed against the governor Orsino's family.

ANTONIO. You're making a mistake, sir.

FIRST OFFICER. No, sir; I know you well, even if you aren't wearing your sea-captain's cap. During a fight at sea, you once seriously injured the governor's nephew. Take him away!

ANTONIO. I must obey. [*to Viola.*] This has happened because I came looking for you. I'm afraid I must ask you to give me back the money I gave you this morning. You seem amazed…

SECOND OFFICER. Come, sir, let's go.

ANTONIO. [*to Viola.*] I must ask you again for my purse.

VIOLA. What money, sir? I wish to thank you for the kindness that you've shown me. I don't have much, but here is half of what I own.

ANTONIO. What? Is it possible that you abandon me now after all that I've done for you?

VIOLA. I know not of these things. Indeed, I don't know you at all.

ANTONIO. I don't believe it!

SECOND OFFICER. Come, sir. It's time to go.

ANTONIO. Please; let me speak a little. This boy, you see, I saved from death; and I came to Illyria only because he asked me, even if I knew that I was in danger of being arrested.

FIRST OFFICER. What's that to us? Let's go! [*leading Antonio away.*]

ANTONIO. Sebastian! You should be ashamed of yourself. Such

good features hide such a cold, ungrateful[1] heart!

[*Exit officers with Antonio.*]

VIOLA. His words are so full of passion, they seem true and I begin to believe him. He called me Sebastian! Could it be that he thought I was my dear brother? Has this man really saved Sebastian's life? Oh! I dare not hope for such joy!

[*Exit Viola.*]

GENTLEMAN. This young man is worse than I thought. Not only has he stolen my sweet Olivia's heart, but he has even abandoned a friend who saved his life in the past. What a coward! I'll look for him again and teach him a lesson.

[*Exit gentleman.*]

Act 4 Scene 1

Another street near Olivia's house.

[*Enter Sebastian, dressed the same as Viola, followed by Olivia's servant.*]

SERVANT. Sir, my lady wishes to speak to you again.

SEBASTIAN. I think you're making a mistake, madam.

SERVANT. Master Cesario, why do you deny your identity? Why do you make my lady suffer so?

SEBASTIAN. Are you mad, woman? Leave me alone.

[*Enter gentleman who had previously challenged Viola.*]

GENTLEMAN. Ah! Sir, I meet you again! Take that! [*striking Sebastian.*]

SEBASTIAN. And take this, and this and this, sir! [*striking the man several times.*] Are all the people here mad?

SERVANT. I must go and tell my lady that Cesario is in a fight.

[*Exit servant. Sebastian and gentleman continue fighting.*]

[*Enter Olivia.*]

OLIVIA. Stop!

GENTLEMAN. Madam! [*stops fighting.*]

OLIVIA [*to gentleman*]. How dare you harm this kind young man. Get

---

1. ungrateful: 忘恩負義

out of my sight!

[*Exit gentleman.*]

OLIVIA. Please, gentle friend, come with me to my house. The man is jealous because you have stolen my heart.

SEBASTIAN. 'Or I am mad, or else this is a dream.'

OLIVIA. Neither. Please come. Won't you do as I ask?

SEBASTIAN. Madam, I will.

OLIVIA. Then, follow me!

[*Exit all.*]

Act 4 Scene 2

Olivia's garden.

[*Enter Sebastian.*]

SEBASTIAN. This is the air, the sun, the garden. Everything is real; I'm not mad, but full of amazement. I wonder where Antonio is. He wasn't in the square, where we arranged to meet. I need his advice. Although reason tells me there must be a mistake, since I've never met this charming lady, my heart wishes it to be true. Or maybe the lady is mad? But she can't be, because she seems wealthy and runs her house and servants well. I don't understand. Ah! Here comes the sweet lady.

[*Enter Olivia and a priest.*]

OLIVIA. Don't blame me for wishing to do things quickly. If you really love me, then come to the church, where this priest will marry us without delay. It'll be our secret until you wish everyone to know. What do you say?

SEBASTIAN. 'I'll follow this good man, and go with you'; and I promise I'll be forever true to you.

OLIVIA [*to priest*]. Then lead the way, good father!

[*Exit all.*]

[*Re-enter Sebastian.*]

SEBASTIAN. What good fortune is this? Now I'm married to a

beautiful wife! While she's resting, I'll go and look for my dear friend, Antonio, to tell him the good news.

[*Exit Sebastian.*]

Act 5 Scene 1

The street outside Olivia's house.

[*Enter Orsino with Viola and Olivia's servant.*]

ORSINO. Do you belong to Lady Olivia's house?

SERVANT. Yes, sir.

ORSINO. Please, let your lady know that I'm here to speak to her.

SERVANT. I'll go immediately, sir.

[*Exit servant.*]

VIOLA. Here comes the man, sir, that rescued me in the street.

[*Enter Antonio with officers.*]

ORSINO. I remember his face. He was captain of a ship during the war. What's the matter?

FIRST OFFICER. Orsino, this is Antonio, that injured your young nephew during a fight at sea.

VIOLA. He was kind to me, sir. He defended me against the gentleman who wished to fight me; but, then, he made a strange speech that made no sense. Maybe he was confused.

ORSINO. Thief and pirate! What made you come to Illyria, where you knew you'd be caught?

ANTONIO. Sir, I've never been a thief or a pirate, but I confess, I've been your enemy in the past. I came here, because of that ungrateful boy by your side. First, I gave him back his life by rescuing him from the rough sea, where he'd have surely drowned. After looking after him, I came here despite the risk for me, but just to please him. Then, I defended him in the street against another man's sword. Then, what did he do? He refused to give me back the purse that I had given him that morning!

VIOLA. How can this be?

ORSINO. When did you come to this town with him?

ANTONIO. Today, my lord; and we've been together for the last three months.

[*Enter Olivia and servant.*]

ORSINO. Here comes Olivia: 'now heaven walks on earth!' As for you, sir; your words are madness; this boy has looked after me for three months. But, we'll talk about this later. Now I must speak to my dear lady.

OLIVIA. Why are you here, my lord?

ORSINO. Sweet Olivia...

OLIVIA. What do you say Cesario? What about your promise to me?

VIOLA. My duty is to say nothing while my lord wishes to speak.

OLIVIA. My lord, Orsino, save your words for someone who is free to love you.

ORSINO. Still so cruel?

OLIVIA. As always with you. My love is only for Cesario.

ORSINO. Cesario! How could you do this to me?

VIOLA. But...

ORSINO. Olivia, I can do you no harm, but I'll take my revenge out on this boy who has stolen his master's love, even if I care for him dearly. Come, Cesario! [*going.*]

VIOLA. Here, I am; I'd die a thousand deaths to give you peace, my lord. [*following.*]

OLIVIA. Where are you going, Cesario?

VIOLA. After the one I love more than my own life; more than I could ever love a wife.

OLIVIA. How can you betray me like this, Cesario?

VIOLA. What do you mean?

OLIVIA. Have you forgotten already? Call the priest!

[*Exit servant.*]

ORSINO. Cesario, come with me!

OLIVIA. Where, my lord? Cesario, my husband, stay!

ORSINO. Husband?

OLIVIA. Yes, husband.

ORSINO. Cesario?

VIOLA. No, my lord, not I.

OLIVIA. Oh Cesario! It must be fear that makes you deny what you are.

[*Enter priest.*]

OLIVIA. Oh, welcome, father! Please tell everyone what, until now, has been a secret. What did you do for this young man and me?

PRIEST. I saw you kiss and exchange rings as a sign of your love, just two hours ago, when I joined you in marriage.

ORSINO. So, all is done and there's no hope for my love. Then, I can but say goodbye, my dear lady; and as for you Cesario, I never want to see you again!

VIOLA. My lord, I must protest…

OLIVIA. Oh Cesario! Are you such a coward as to deny everything?

[*Enter Sebastian.*]

SEBASTIAN. My sweet wife, Olivia! Why such a strange expression? Have I been away too long?

ORSINO. One face, one voice, same clothes, and two people. It can't be!

SEBASTIAN. Antonio! Oh my dear Antonio!

ANTONIO. Sebastian, is it you?

SEBASTIAN. Are you afraid of me?

ANTONIO. How have you managed to divide yourself? These two creatures are identical. Which is Sebastian?

SEBASTIAN [*seeing Viola*]. But, I never had a brother. Only a sister, who drowned in a storm at sea. Please, tell me, are we relatives?

VIOLA. I'm from Messaline: my father's name was Sebastian; and Sebastian was also my brother's name. He drowned at sea.

SEBASTIAN. If you were a woman, I would cry for joy, and welcome my poor drowned Viola.

VIOLA. Oh! My dear brother! Don't be fooled by my appearance. Come with me to my friend, the sea captain, who saved me from the waves. He'll tell you that I'm Viola, and that I dressed as a boy to become Orsino's messenger.

SEBASTIAN. Oh! Happiness! My sister is alive. [to Olivia.] So you've been tricked, my lady; you almost married my sister! [laughing.]

OLIVIA. Yes! But happily, now I have a wonderful husband and a sweet sister.

ORSINO. I too am amazed, and can hardly believe it; they are so alike. [to Viola.] Boy, you told me a thousand times that my love for a woman could never be as strong as your love for me.

VIOLA. And still it is so, my lord, my secret love!

ORSINO. Give me your hand then. [kisses hand.]

OLIVIA. Orsino, now that, you too, have found true love, I offer you my house and my priest, so you and Viola can be happily married like Sebastian and I.

ORSINO. Madam, if my sweet Viola agrees, I'll be delighted to accept your offer.

VIOLA. Of course I agree, my love!

ORSINO. Then, let's go and be married; then all together, we can celebrate the happy events of this extraordinary day.

[Exit all.]

Stop & Check

1 **Put these events from *Twelfth Night* into chronological order from 1 to 10.**

A ☐ Olivia declares her love to Cesario.

B ☐ A gentleman challenges Viola to fight.

C ☐ Viola becomes Orsino's messenger.

D ☐ Sebastian marries Olivia.

E ☐ Orsino marries Viola.

F ☐ Olivia gives her servant a ring for Cesario.

G ☐ Antonio defends Viola.

H ☐ A gentleman strikes Sebastian.

I ☐ The officers bring Antonio to Orsino.

J ☐ Antonio is arrested.

Writing

2a **Write a short summary explaining the love triangle in *Twelfth Night*. Consider the following:**

• who is involved in the love triangle.

• how disguise plays an important part.

• how everything is solved in the end.

_____

_____

_____

_____

_____

_____

_____

2b **Now answer these questions.**

1 Did you enjoy the play? Why/why not?

2 How would you change the story so that Orsino marries Olivia in the end?

3 Which character would you like to play in *Twelfth Night*? Why?

Grammar

3 **Complete the sentences with the correct form of the verb in brackets. Be careful of affirmative or negative forms; the sentence must make sense.**

1 If there hadn't been a storm, the ship _____ (sink)

2 No-one will ever discover Viola is a girl unless the captain _____ (say) something.

3 If Viola and Sebastian _____ (be) identical twins, people wouldn't get confused.

4 Antonio wishes he _____ (lend) the money to Sebastian.

5 No sooner _____ (Sebastian /start) to fight with the gentleman, than Olivia stopped them.

6 Orsino _____ (write) love letters to Olivia for months, but she is not interested.

7 Antonio _____ (arrest) if he hadn't returned to Illyria.

8 Orsino wishes Olivia _____ (give) him a chance to show his love to her.

PRE-READING ACTIVITY

Vocabulary

4 **The next play, *Macbeth*, is the shortest of Shakespeare's tragedies. Read the definitions and complete the words which are all in this tragedy.**

1 A fight between armies   b _ _ _ _ _

2 An action against the law   c _ _ _ _

3 To kill   m _ _ _ _ _

4 To hit violently   s _ _ _ _ _

5 A red liquid in humans   b _ _ _ _

6 Bad   e _ _ _

Macbeth

Characters:

DUNCAN,	*King of Scotland.*
MALCOLM,	*Duncan's sons.*
DONALBAIN,	
MACBETH,	*Scottish captain and King Duncan's cousin.*
LADY MACBETH,	*Macbeth's wife.*
BANQUO,	*Scottish captain.*
FLEANCE,	*Banquo's son.*
MACDUFF,	*Lord of Fife.*
3 WITCHES.	
2 MURDERERS.	
MESSENGER.	
SERVANT.	
3 SPIRITS.	
SOLDIERS AND LORDS.	

 Two Scottish captains, Macbeth and Banquo, are returning home after bravely fighting for their King of Scotland, Duncan, in a terrible battle against the Norwegians.

Act 1 Scene 1

A lonely area in the Scottish countryside. Thunder.

[*Enter Macbeth and Banquo.*]

MACBETH. Such bad weather on such a fortunate day has never been seen.

BANQUO. It can't be far now to Forres where our king is. But, look! What are those strange, wild, old creatures coming this way? They look like women, but they have beards!

[*Enter three witches.*]

MACBETH. Speak if you can: what are you?

FIRST WITCH. Macbeth! I greet you, Lord of Glamis!

SECOND WITCH. Macbeth! I greet you, Lord of Cawdor!

THIRD WITCH. Macbeth! You'll become King of Scotland.

[*Macbeth is shocked by these words.*]

BANQUO. Macbeth, why do you seem to fear these fantastic predictions of such good fortune? [*to the witches.*] What of me, Banquo? What can you tell me?

FIRST WITCH. You're lesser than Macbeth, and greater.

SECOND WITCH. Not so happy, but much happier.

THIRD WITCH. You'll never become King of Scotland, but your sons will. Now we must go.

MACBETH. Stay and tell me more: it's true I'm lord of Glamis, but not of Cawdor. The Lord of Cawdor is still alive; and I have no right to become king. So, why do you say these things?

[*The witches disappear as Macbeth is speaking.*]

BANQUO. Where have they gone?

MACBETH. Into the air, like the wind.

BANQUO. Did we imagine it all?

MACBETH. Your children will be kings.

BANQUO. You'll be king.

MACBETH. And Lord of Cawdor too; is that what they said?

BANQUO. The exact words. But, look! A messenger.

[*Enter Messenger.*]

MESSENGER. The king has received news of your success in battle, Macbeth. He thanks you for your bravery, and wishes you to be known as Lord of Cawdor from now on.

BANQUO. What! Can the devil speak true?

MACBETH. But the Lord of Cawdor is still alive.

MESSENGER. True; but he has betrayed the king, and lost his name and honour; so, you'll take his place.

MACBETH [*aside*]. Glamis, and Lord of Cawdor. [*to Banquo.*] Don't you now hope your children will become kings, since the witches have been right so far?

BANQUO. That same hope might make you want to become king. Witches often tell us little truths which trick us into doing things that have much more serious consequences.

MACBETH [*aside*]. Two truths have been told so far. The witches' predictions can't be evil if they started with a truth. I'm now Lord of Cawdor. To become king, though, means Duncan must be murdered.

BANQUO [*to messenger*]. Look how Macbeth is lost in thought. Macbeth, we're waiting for you.

MACBETH. I'm sorry, my mind was elsewhere. Come, friends, let's go to the king.

[*Exit all.*]

Act 1 Scene 2

Forres. A room in King Duncan's palace.

[*Enter Duncan, Malcolm, Donalbain, Macbeth and Banquo.*]

DUNCAN. My worthiest cousin, Macbeth! How grateful I am to you for defending your country; and you too Banquo!

MACBETH. Our duty is to protect our state and king. We're your loyal servants.

DUNCAN. You fill me with joy. Let's go to your castle in Inverness, Macbeth, and celebrate.

MACBETH. I'll go now and tell my wife of your approach.

DUNCAN. Let's follow our dear loyal friend, to his home.

[*Exit all.*]

Act 1 Scene 3

Inverness. Macbeth's castle.

[*Enter Lady Macbeth, reading a letter from Macbeth about his strange meeting with the witches.*]

LADY MACBETH. [*commenting on the letter to herself*]. Lord of Glamis and Cawdor; and you'll also be what you were promised, King of Scotland! But, I fear your nature; you're too full of human kindness. You'd be the greatest if only you were more ambitious. Come home quickly my husband, so I can give you courage to become king.

[*Enter Macbeth.*]

LADY MACBETH. Great Glamis! Worthy Cawdor! Your letter makes me hope for a great future.

MACBETH. My dearest love, Duncan is coming here tonight.

LADY MACBETH. And when does he plan to leave again?

MACBETH. Tomorrow.

LADY MACBETH. Then, he'll never see tomorrow's sunrise. All you have to do is welcome Duncan; I'll do the rest.

[*Exit all.*]

Act 1 Scene 4

A room in Macbeth's castle. Duncan has arrived with his sons. Macbeth is having doubts about the plan to murder his king.

[*Enter Macbeth.*]

MACBETH. Duncan has always trusted me, and even more so now, that he's my guest. My duty is to protect him against murderers, not hold the knife in my own hand. Such a fair king!

[*Enter Lady Macbeth.*]

LADY MACBETH. Why did you leave the room? Duncan has almost finished eating and will go to bed soon.

MACBETH. 'We will proceed no further in this business': I've received many honours from Duncan, and people admire and respect me; I don't wish to lose all of this.

LADY MACBETH. Where has all your courage gone?

MACBETH. What if we fail?

LADY MACBETH. We fail! But if you have courage, then we won't fail. When Duncan is asleep, I'll give his servants our best food and wine until they're so full, that they too will fall asleep. Then, we can kill Duncan, and his servants will be blamed for not protecting him.

MACBETH. I have an even better plan; we'll mark the servants with Duncan's blood and use their daggers[1], so everyone will think they've done the crime.

LADY MACBETH. What a brilliant mind, my love.

MACBETH. Then, it's settled; all will be done. Until then, 'false face must hide what the false heart doth know'.

[*Exit all.*]

Act 2 Scene 1

Inverness. The castle gardens.

[*Enter Banquo.*]

BANQUO. It's after midnight.

[*Enter Macbeth with a candle.*]

BANQUO. Who's there?

MACBETH. A friend.

BANQUO. What sir! Are you still up? Before going to bed, the king told me to give you this valuable diamond for your wife, to thank her for all her kindness.

MACBETH. He's our guest, so we do only our duty.

BANQUO. All's well then. Last night, I dreamt of the three strange sisters.

---

1. daggers: 匕首

MACBETH. 'I think not of them.' Goodnight, my friend; sleep well.

BANQUO. You too.

[*Exit Banquo.*]

A bell rings.

MACBETH. I'll go and do it. The bell invites me. Hear not the bell, Duncan, that calls you to heaven or to hell.

[*Exit Macbeth.*]

Act 2 Scene 2

A room in the castle.

[*Enter Lady Macbeth.*]

LADY MACBETH. The wine that made the servants sleep, gave me courage. I thought to kill the king myself, with their daggers, rather than leaving Macbeth to do it. But, as he slept, Duncan looked so like my father that my courage left me.

[*Enter Macbeth, confused, with two daggers covered in blood.*]

LADY MACBETH. My husband!

MACBETH. I've done it. [*looking at his hands covered in blood.*] This is a sad sight.

LADY MACBETH. What a foolish thought!

MACBETH. One of the servants laughed in his sleep, and the other one cried 'Murder!' as if he could see me with my hands covered in Duncan's blood.

LADY MACBETH. Think no more about your actions, or you'll go mad.

MACBETH. I thought I heard a voice cry 'Macbeth will sleep no more!'

LADY MACBETH. But who cried, my lord? Stop talking such nonsense. Put the daggers back beside the servants, and put some blood on their cheeks, so they'll be accused of the murder. Then, wash the blood from your hands.

MACBETH. I can't go back into that room. I'm afraid even to think of what I've done; I dare not look at it again.

LADY MACBETH. You're hopeless! Give me the daggers. 'The sleeping and the dead are but as pictures.' I'll do it! Then we'll go to bed.

[*Exit all.*]

Act 2 Scene 3

Inverness. A room in the castle.

The next morning.

[*Enter Macbeth and Macduff.*]

MACBETH. Good morning, sir.

MACDUFF. Good morning. Is the king already awake, my lord?

MACBETH. Not yet.

MACDUFF. I'll go and call him, as he wishes to leave early today.

MACBETH. And I'll call my servants.

[*Exit all.*]

[*Re-enter Macduff, quickly followed by Macbeth.*]

MACDUFF. Oh horror! Horror! Horror!

MACBETH. What's the matter?

MACDUFF. Our king has been murdered.

MACBETH. What? It can't be!

MACDUFF. Go to his room and see for yourself.

[*Exit Macbeth.*]

MACDUFF. Ring the alarm bell. Banquo, Malcolm, Donalbain! Awake and see this horror.

[*Enter Lady Macbeth.*]

LADY MACBETH. What's all this noise?

MACDUFF. Oh gentle lady! What I have to say might kill you.

[*Enter Banquo.*]

MACDUFF. Oh Banquo! Banquo! Our royal master has been murdered!

LADY MACBETH. Oh no! What? In our house?

BANQUO. Anywhere is too cruel. Dear Macduff, please tell me it isn't true.

[*Re-enter Macbeth.*]

MACBETH. If I had died just one hour ago, I'd have lived a happier life, without this bloody sight.

[*Enter Malcolm and Donalbain.*]

DONALBAIN. What's the matter?

MACBETH. Your royal father has been murdered. It looks as if his servants did it. Their daggers and faces were covered in blood.

LADY MACBETH. Help me!

MACDUFF. Watch the lady! She's fainting!

MALCOM [*aside to Donalbain*]. We're in danger. Let's run away, before they kill us too.

BANQUO. See to your wife Macbeth, then let's all meet in the hall together.

[*Macbeth carries out Lady Macbeth.*]

[*Exit all except Malcolm and Donalbain.*]

MALCOM. I'm going to England.

DONALBAIN. And I to Ireland. We'll be safer if we aren't together.

MALCOM. The hand that killed our father has not finished its work yet. So, let's go now before anyone sees us.

[*Exit all.*]

Act 3 Scene 1

Forres. A room in the King's Palace.

[*Since Malcolm and Donalbain have run away, Macbeth has become king.*]

[*Enter Banquo.*]

BANQUO. He has it all now: King, Cawdor, Glamis, just as the witches promised. I fear that Macbeth has played dirty games to satisfy his ambition. But the witches also said that my children, not his, would be the future kings of Scotland. If all has come true for him, then why not for me too? But, Hush!

[*Enter Macbeth as king, and Lady Macbeth as queen.*]

MACBETH [*indicating Banquo*]. Here's our most important guest!

LADY MACBETH: He must be with us tonight, or we'll miss him terribly.

MACBETH. Tonight, we're having a special supper with all our lords, sir, and I request your presence.

BANQUO. It's my duty to obey you, my king.

MACBETH. We've heard that Malcolm and Donalbain, are hiding in England, suspected of being involved in the bloody crime against their own father. What's more, they're spreading strange rumours about me; but we'll talk about that tomorrow. Are you going riding now?

BANQUO. Yes, my lord.

MACBETH. Is your dear son Fleance going with you?

BANQUO. He is, my lord.

MACBETH. Well, ride well and return in time for supper.

BANQUO. My lord, I will.

LADY MACBETH: I'll go with you to your horse, sir, to wish your son well.

[*Exit Lady Macbeth and Banquo.*]

MACBETH. 'Our fears in Banquo stick deep.' The witches said he'd be the father to a line of kings. Now that I'm king, I'm forced to take action to write a new fate. This time, though, I won't dirty my own hands with Banquo's blood. We have too many friends in common, whose love and respect I wish to keep.

[*Exit Macbeth.*]

Act 3 Scene 2

Forres. Another room in the Palace.

[*Enter Macbeth with two murderers.*]

MACBETH. I need your help.

FIRST MURDERER. Command, my lord.

MACBETH. Tonight, hide and wait on the road to the palace. When Banquo and his son Fleance pass, strike them both until dead.

SECOND MURDERER. Consider it done, my lord.

[*Exit all.*]

Act 3 Scene 3

A park with a road, leading to the palace.

[*Enter the two murderers.*]

FIRST MURDERER. Listen! I hear horses.

SECOND MURDERER. Wait until they leave their horses and start to walk towards the palace gates.

FIRST MURDERER. Here they come. I can see a light.

[*Enter Banquo and Fleance. The murderers attack Banquo.*]

BANQUO. Run, Fleance, run! Run! [*dies.*]

[*Exit Fleance running.*]

FIRST MURDERER. Only one is down. The son has escaped.

SECOND MURDERER. We must tell Macbeth.

[*Exit murderers.*]

Act 3 Scene 4

Forres. A big dining room in the Palace. Table ready for supper.

[*Enter Macbeth, Lady Macbeth, Macduff and other lords and servants.*]

MACBETH. Welcome, my lords. Let's sit and eat.

MACDUFF. Thank you, my lord.

[*Enter first murderer. He waits at the door for Macbeth. Macbeth gets up to speak to him.*]

MACBETH. There's blood on your face. Is it Banquo's?

FIRST MURDERER. Yes, my lord, but Fleance got away.

MACBETH. So, doubts and fears will stay in my mind! Go, and we'll speak tomorrow. Now I must return to my guests.

[*Exit first murderer.*]

[*Banquo's ghost enters, and sits in Macbeth's place at the table. Macbeth turns round to go back to his place and sees Banquo's ghost. Only he can see it.*]

MACBETH. The table is full.

MACDUFF. Here's your place, my worthy lord.

MACBETH. Where? Which of you has done this?

LADY MACBETH. What, my lord?

MACBETH. Don't shake your bloody hair at me.

LADY MACBETH. Calm yourself. It's your fear that makes you see strange things. Why such a face? You're looking at an empty chair.

MACBETH. Look! There he is!

[*The ghost disappears.*]

MACBETH. 'Murders have been performed too terrible for the ear.' Before, men died, but now they rise again and take our seats.

LADY MACBETH. My worthy lord, your guests need you.

MACBETH. Sorry, my friends. I have a strange illness. Those who know me think nothing of it. Let's drink to us all, and to our dear friend Banquo. If only he were here too!

[*They all stand and raise their glasses.*]

[*Re-enter Banquo's ghost.*]

MACBETH. Get out of my sight! Hide under the earth! Your blood is cold. Why are you staring at me with those eyes that can see nothing?

LADY MACBETH. You're spoiling the happy evening for all.

[*Ghost disappears.*]

MACBETH. How can you see such a sight and not be white with fear like me?

MACDUFF. What sight, my lord?

LADY MACBETH. Please, ask no questions. He's getting worse and worse. I beg you all to leave at once. Goodnight, my friends.

[*Exit all except Macbeth and Lady Macbeth.*]

MACBETH. How late is it?

LADY MACBETH. Still night. But morning will soon be here.

MACBETH. Then, I'll go and look for the strange witches. I need to know the worst.

LADY MACBETH. Come and sleep first.

MACBETH. I can't sleep. My dreams are full of blood.

[*Exit all.*]

Act 4 Scene 1

A cave. In the middle, a boiling cauldron[1].

[*Thunder. Enter the three witches.*]

FIRST WITCH. Round about the cauldron go. Into it, every poison throw.

SECOND WITCH. The tail of the rat.

THIRD WITCH. The skin of the snake.

ALL. And now let's sing and dance around the cauldron, so the magic will begin. 'Double, double, toil and trouble; Fire burn and cauldron bubble.'

[*Enter Macbeth.*]

MACBETH. What are you doing, you secret, evil creatures of the night?

FIRST WITCH. What we do has no name.

MACBETH. I beg you, answer my questions.

FIRST WITCH. Speak.

SECOND WITCH. Demand.

THIRD WITCH. We'll answer, if you want, through the mouths of our masters, the spirits.

MACBETH. Call them. Let me see them.

FIRST SPIRIT. Macbeth! Macbeth! Be on your guard, Macduff, Lord of Fife, is dangerous.

MACBETH. Then, he must die.

SECOND SPIRIT. Macbeth! Macbeth! Be bloody and fearless. No man born of a woman can harm Macbeth.

THIRD SPIRIT. Be like a lion, proud and not cautious. Macbeth will

1. cauldron: 大鍋

never be defeated until Great Birnam wood on Dunsinane Hill moves.

MACBETH. That will never be. Who can make all the trees in the forest come out the ground and walk? I see that I'll live a long life and not die a violent death. But, answer just one more question; will Banquo's children ever become kings of Scotland?

ALL. Ask no more.

[*The spirits disappear. The cauldron starts to sink into the ground and music can be heard.*]

THE THREE WITCHES. Show! Show! Show!

[*Macbeth sees eight kings, followed by Banquo's ghost, covered in blood.*]

MACBETH. You dirty witches! Why do you show me these things? Banquo's children and their children, all kings!

FIRST WITCH. Yes sir, all this is so. But why are you so amazed? Come sisters, our duties are done.

[*The three witches disappear.*]

MACBETH. Come back!

[*Enter messenger.*]

MESSENGER. My lord, Macduff has run away to England to join Malcolm's army to fight against you.

MACBETH [*furious*]. To England! He has escaped his fate for now, but he'll suffer just the same. He'll lose his family for betraying me.

[*Exit all.*]

Act 4 Scene 2

England. Outside the King's palace.

[*Enter Malcolm and Macduff.*]

MALCOLM. Sir, I fear our country is sinking; it cries and bleeds at the hands of Macbeth.

MACDUFF. There has never been anyone as evil as Macbeth.

MALCOLM. Thousands here in England are ready to fight against him. His bloody actions have made him many enemies.

MACDUFF. Then, fight to become King of Scotland, my lord.

MALCOLM. I will.

[*Enter Messenger.*]

MESSENGER. I come with news from Scotland.

MALCOLM. Is it still standing?

MESSENGER. Just; you're needed to fight against Macbeth.

MALCOLM. We're coming now with thousands of men from England.

MESSENGER. I wish this news would take away my grief.

MACDUFF. What worries you?

MESSENGER. Your worries.

MACDUFF. Speak sir!

MESSENGER. Your castle in Fife was surprised, and your wife and children killed at the hands of Macbeth's murderers.

MACDUFF [*falling to his knees*]. My children too?

MESSENGER. Wife, children, servants, all that could be found.

MACDUFF. Let grief guide my sword till I destroy Macbeth and all his men.

MALCOLM. Yes, let revenge cure your grief. Come! It's time for Macbeth to fall.

[*Exit all.*]

Act 5 Scene 1

Dunsinane. A room in the Castle.

[*Enter Lady Macbeth, dressed for bed; eyes open, but as if walking in her sleep.*]

LADY MACBETH [*as if washing her hands*]. The blood stays, it won't go away. 'Yet who would have thought the old man to have had so much blood in him?' The Lord of Fife had a wife: where is she now? Will these hands of mine never be clean? To bed, to bed. 'What's done cannot be undone.'

[*Exit.*]

Act 5 Scene 2

Dunsinane. Another room in the castle.

[Enter Macbeth, sad and tired.]

MACBETH. Perhaps I've lived long enough. Honour, love and friends should be companions of old age; but I have none of these.

[Enter a servant.]

SERVANT. My lord, thousands of English soldiers are on their way here.

MACBETH *[furious once more]*. Then, I'll fight till I die! Go and look for more men to fight for me. Hang those who refuse. How is my Lady Macbeth?

SERVANT. Disturbed by blood-filled dreams.

MACBETH. Tell the doctor to find a cure. Now let's get ready to fight!

[Exit all.]

Act 5 Scene 3

Countryside near Birnam Wood.

[Enter Malcolm, Macduff and soldiers.]

MALCOLM. One day soon, this land will be safe.

MACDUFF. We're sure it will, with you leading us, my lord.

MALCOLM. Now, my men; each of you must take a branch from a tree and hide behind it as you walk. In this way, Macbeth and his men won't be able to count how many we are.

MACDUFF. We know only that Macbeth is still in Dunsinane.

MALCOLM. Then let's proceed towards his castle and meet him in battle.

[Exit all.]

Act 5 Scene 4

Dunsinane. Inside the castle.

[Enter Macbeth.]

MACBETH. Let them come. My castle is strong. I'll wait until hunger and illness eat them.

[*The scream of a woman from somewhere inside the castle.*]

MACBETH. What's that noise?

[*Enter a servant.*]

SERVANT. My lord; the queen is dead.

MACBETH. Death has come too soon to her. 'Out, out, brief candle!' Life is a story, told by an idiot, full of noise and anger, meaning nothing.

[*Enter a messenger.*]

MESSENGER. My lord, I must say what I saw, but don't know how to.

MACBETH. Well, speak, sir.

MESSENGER. I was standing on the hill, looking towards Birnam and suddenly the wood started to move.

MACBETH. Liar!

MESSENGER. Believe me, my lord. Look, and you'll see it coming.

MACBETH. 'Fear not till Birnam wood comes to Dunsinane' is what the spirits said, and now it has come true. But I won't run away. Ring the alarm bell! Let's go and fight till we can!

[*Exit all.*]

Act 5 Scene 5

Outside, near the castle.

[*Enter Macbeth.*]

MACBETH. I'm trapped; but the spirits said I should fear only he not born by a woman. No such man exists, so I need not fear.

[*Exit Macbeth.*]

[*Enter Malcolm and Macduff.*]

MACDUFF. This way, my lord; the castle is ours.

MALCOLM. I'll respect my father's name and be a good king to our people.

[*Exit all.*]

[*Re-enter Macbeth.*]

MACBETH. I can still fight. I won't kill myself with my own sword.

[*Re-enter Macduff. He sees Macbeth standing with his back to him.*]

MACDUFF. Turn round, evil snake from hell!

MACBETH. I've fought with all men except you. Enough of this blood!

MACDUFF. 'I have no words. My voice is my sword.'

[*They fight.*]

MACBETH. Your sword is useless; I can't be killed by a man born of a woman.

MACDUFF. Hear me, as I say that I was not born in the ordinary manner that men are born, but was taken from my mother suddenly, before the natural time for such an event was up.

MACBETH. The evil spirits can be believed no more. So, let's fight Macduff!

[*Exit Macbeth and Macduff fighting.*]

[*Enter Malcolm and soldiers.*]

MALCOLM. Are we all safe? Where's Macduff?

[*Re-enter Macduff, with Macbeth's head on his sword.*]

MACDUFF. My king! Here's Macbeth's head. Our kingdom is free. Long live Malcolm, King of Scotland!

MALCOLM. Thanks to you all, we're free from this butcher and his evil wife. You're all invited to Scone where with great ceremony I'll officially be named King of Scotland.

[*Exit all.*]

AFTER-READING ACTIVITIES

Stop & Check

1 Answer the following questions about the play, *Macbeth*.

1 Who does Macbeth meet while returning from battle?
2 How important is this meeting for the plot?
3 Who is Macbeth's first victim? Why?
4 Whose ghost appears to Macbeth and when?
5 How does the character of Lady Macbeth change and what happens to her in the end?
6 How does the witches' prediction about Birnam Wood come true?
7 Who becomes King of Scotland at the end of the play?

Grammar

2 Transform the sentences about the play into the passive.

1 At the start of the play, the Scottish army had defeated the Norwegians.
2 King Duncan thanked Macbeth for his bravery in battle.
3 Lady Macbeth will encourage Macbeth to carry out his evil plan.
4 The king gave Lady Macbeth a diamond for her kindness.
5 Macbeth has invited Banquo to a special dinner.
6 They are serving dinner when Banquo's ghost appears.
7 While the murderers were attacking Banquo, his son ran away.
8 People used to admire and respect Macbeth.
9 Macbeth will mark the servants with Duncan's blood.
10 The witches are going to call the spirits for Macbeth.

Writing

3a *'Macbeth is a tragic hero, ruined by ambition.'* Do you agree or disagree with this statement? Write a short paragraph (10 lines) explaining your opinion.

3b Now, answer these questions.

1 Are you ambitious? Why/Why not?
2 When do you think it might be an advantage to be ambitious?
3 What are the negative aspects of being too ambitious?
4 What adjectives would you use to describe your character?
5 What qualities do you look for in a friend?

PRE-READING ACTIVITY

Speaking

4 Listen to Act 1 Scene 1 of the next play, *Much Ado About Nothing*. Are these statements true (T) or false (F)?

	T	F
1 Beatrice is Leonato's daughter.	☐	☐
2 Leonato already knows the soldiers who arrive at his palace.	☐	☐
3 Benedick and Beatrice never argue with each other.	☐	☐
4 Claudio is busy listening to Benedick.	☐	☐
5 Leonato agrees with Don Pedro's opinion.	☐	☐
6 Don Pedro will speak in Claudio's favour to Leonato.	☐	☐

Much Ado About Nothing

Characters:

LEONATO,	*Governor of Messina.*
HERO,	*Leonato's daughter.*
BEATRICE,	*Leonato's niece.*
DON PEDRO,	*Prince of Arragon.*
CLAUDIO,	*a young lord of Florence.*
BENEDICK,	*a young lord of Padua.*
URSULA AND MARGARET,	*Hero's servants.*
DON JOHN,	*Pedro's half-brother.*
BORACHIO,	*one of Don John's men.*
FRIAR FRANCIS,	*a kind of priest.*

Hero, a young serious lady, lives with her father Leonato and her lively young cousin Beatrice, in her father's palace in Messina. Beatrice is full of fun and witty[1], unlike the shy Hero. One day, some army officers come to visit Leonato at his palace, after fighting bravely in the war. They're old friends of his; Pedro, the Prince of Arragon, his friend Claudio a lord from Florence, and a lord from Padua called Benedick, who's also witty like Beatrice. Indeed, they're so alike, that Benedick and Beatrice quarrel every time they see each other.

1. **witty:** 機智

Act 1 Scene 1

Messina. A room in Leonato's palace.

[*Enter Leonato, Hero, Beatrice, Don Pedro, Claudio and Benedick.*]

LEONATO. Welcome to my home. We're honoured to have the company of such brave soldiers.

BENEDICK. Yes indeed; we spent many days and nights in heavy battle, but all misery is forgotten at the sight of your sweet daughter.

[*Beatrice, bored by Benedick, decides to interrupt him.*]

BEATRICE. I'm amazed you're still talking, Lord Benedick. No-one is listening to you.

BENEDICK. Oh my dear lady Criticism, are you still alive?

BEATRICE. How can my criticism die in your presence? Kindness itself is forced to criticise when you appear.

BENEDICK. Then kindness betrays itself. My lady, 'I wish my horse had the speed of your tongue.'

BEATRICE. As always, you end with a silly comment like a clown, my lord.

[*Meanwhile, Claudio is secretly watching Hero, and realises that she has become a beautiful young lady since he last saw her. The prince instead, has been listening carefully to Beatrice and Benedick's conversation.*]

DON PEDRO [*whispering to Leonato*]. Beatrice is very witty. She'd make an excellent wife for Benedick.

LEONATO. Oh, my lord, I can't imagine a worse couple.

DON PEDRO. No, my lord. These two witty minds would be perfect together.

LEONATO. Well, let's go into the garden. The fresh air will cool their anger.

[*Exit all, except Don Pedro who is stopped by Claudio.*]

CLAUDIO. Don Pedro, may I speak to you?

DON PEDRO. What secret do you hold, my lord?

CLAUDIO. Did you notice Leonato's daughter? Isn't she a sweet young lady?

DON PEDRO. Why all these questions about Hero, my dear Claudio?

CLAUDIO. For my eyes, she's the sweetest lady I've ever seen.

DON PEDRO. Do you love her? For the lady deserves great love and respect.

CLAUDIO. Yes, for sure I love her.

DON PEDRO. And I'm sure she's worthy of your love. Tonight at dinner, I'll speak to Hero of your love for her. Then, I'll convince her father Leonato of your noble[1] intentions.

[*Exit Don Pedro and Claudio.*]

Act 2 Scene 1

Hall in Leonato's house.

[*Enter Don Pedro, Claudio and Beatrice.*]

DON PEDRO. Claudio, why such a sad face?

CLAUDIO. I'm not sad, my lord.

DON PEDRO. Are you sick then?

BEATRICE. He's neither, my lord; he's jealous. He saw Hero smiling at you and thinks she loves you.

DON PEDRO. Don't fear; her smile was for you Claudio. I've spoken of you kindly to Hero and won her heart for you. I've also convinced her father, Leonato, of your noble intentions, and he has agreed for you to marry his sweet daughter. All that remains, is to name the wedding day. Here come Leonato and Hero now.

[*Enter Leonato and Hero.*]

LEONATO. Claudio, I happily give you my daughter's hand.

BEATRICE. Say something, Claudio!

CLAUDIO. I'm so happy and honoured, that no words can express how much joy I feel.

[*The shy Hero smiles at Claudio and whispers in his ear.*]

---

1. **noble:** 高尚

CLAUDIO. Oh joy! She too loves me!

BEATRICE. Cousin, I wish you every happiness. I'll go now, just in case I too become love-sick. I'd never forgive you for giving me such a ridiculous illness.

[*Exit Beatrice.*]

DON PEDRO. So, Claudio, when do you wish to marry?

CLAUDIO. Tomorrow!

LEONATO. I fear you must wait until Monday, just a week away, and hardly enough time to prepare everything.

DON PEDRO. And to pass the time Claudio, you can help me make Benedick and Beatrice fall in love with each other. I'm sure they'll make a handsome couple.

CLAUDIO. As you wish, my lord.

LEONATO. I'll also help you, my lord.

DON PEDRO. And you too, gentle Hero?

HERO. I'll do all I can, my lord, to help my cousin find a noble husband.

DON PEDRO. Excellent! Hero, you'll help by convincing Beatrice that Benedick is in love with her. Instead, with your help, Leonato and Claudio, we'll make Benedick believe that Beatrice loves him. Come now, and I'll tell you how.

[*Exit all.*]

Act 2 Scene 2

Leonato's garden.

[*Enter Benedick with a book in his hand.*]

BENEDICK. I'll sit and read quietly here in the garden. Ah! Here comes Don Pedro and the love-sick Claudio. I'll hide behind the trees in the orchard[1]. I don't wish to hear of boring wedding plans.

[*Enter Don Pedro, Leonato and Claudio. They've been watching Benedick and know he's hiding in the orchard, but they pretend not to see him. They stop and start talking where they know he'll hear them.*]

1. orchard: 果園

DON PEDRO. The garden is beautiful and peaceful at this time of day.

CLAUDIO. Yes, my lord. Not a soul in sight.

DON PEDRO. Leonato; what was it that you were saying the other day, that your niece Beatrice is in love with Benedick?

CLAUDIO. I never thought Beatrice would love any man.

LEONATO. Neither did I; especially Benedick. She always speaks as if she hates him.

DON PEDRO. Maybe she's just joking when she says she loves him.

CLAUDIO. No, her passion for Benedick is true. Hero told me that Beatrice is so in love with Benedick that she'll die of grief if he can't learn to love her too.

BENEDICK [*aside*]. Is it possible? Or is it the wind playing tricks on me?

DON PEDRO. Has she told Benedick of this new-found love for him?

LEONATO. No; and she says she never will.

CLAUDIO. She says that she has been so nasty to Benedick in the past, that now she's ashamed to declare her love to him.

DON PEDRO. Then someone else should tell Benedick?

CLAUDIO. No! He'll surely laugh and make some witty comment.

DON PEDRO. If he did, I'd have him hanged for such cruelty. Beatrice is an excellent, sweet lady.

CLAUDIO. And she's so wise.

DON PEDRO. In everything except in loving Benedick. I feel so sorry for your niece, Leonato. Let's go and tell Benedick.

LEONATO. No, my lord. Beatrice will die of shame.

DON PEDRO. Well, we'll speak again to your daughter Hero.

LEONATO. Let's go inside now since the air is cool.

DON PEDRO [*aside*]. Now, Hero and her servants must prepare the same trap for Beatrice.

CLAUDIO [*aside*]. Benedick must surely love sweet Beatrice now, after all he has heard.

[Exit Don Pedro, Claudio and Leonato.]

[Benedick comes out of the orchard.]

BENEDICK. This can be no trick. The truth came from Hero. Beatrice loves me! They say I'm proud. Well, now I know my faults, I can mend my ways. I'll be horribly in love with her. I never thought I'd marry, but people change all the time. After all that has been said, I'm a monster if I don't love her. I'll go and look for her now.

[Exit Benedick.]

Act 3 Scene 1

Leonato's garden.

[Enter Hero, Margaret and Ursula.]

HERO. Margaret, run to the hall, and tell my cousin Beatrice that Ursula and I are talking about her in the garden. Advise her to come and hide among the dark shadows of the orchard, where she can listen undisturbed to what we're saying.

MARGARET. I'll make her come, my lady, I promise.

[Exit Margaret.]

HERO. Now Ursula, when Beatrice comes, we'll walk along this path near the orchard, where she'll hide and be able to hear us. We'll talk only of Benedick, and when I name him, you must praise him much more than he deserves. I, instead, will talk about how Benedick is in love with Beatrice.

URSULA. I'll do all you ask of me, my lady.

HERO. Look, here comes Beatrice now. Let's start!

[Enter Beatrice. She sees Hero and Ursula deep in conversation, and hides in the orchard where she can hear what they're saying.]

HERO. To be honest Ursula, she's so arrogant[1] at times.

URSULA. But are you sure that Benedick is really in love with Beatrice? He's such a witty, noble, young man. How lucky she is!

HERO. Well, that's what the prince and Claudio say. They begged me

1. **arrogant:** 高傲

to tell Beatrice, but I said that, if they're really Benedick's friends, they should never tell her.

URSULA. Certainly; it's better that she doesn't know of his love, for she'd make fun of the poor man.

HERO. Indeed; I've never heard her praise any man, no matter how wise, noble or handsome he is. Beatrice is always so proud and her witty comments are often too sharp.

URSULA. But surely she wouldn't refuse such a rare gentleman as Lord Benedick.

HERO. Well, he's the best man in Italy, after my dear Claudio, of course.

URSULA. Ah, yes, lord Claudio. When is your wedding day, my lady?

HERO. Tomorrow. Come with me now to my room, and help me choose what to wear.

URSULA. Certainly, my lady.

[*Exit Hero and Ursula.*]

[*Beatrice comes out of the orchard.*]

BEATRICE. What fire is in my ears? Can this be true? Gone forever are my insults, my criticism and my pride. Benedick, love me still, and my wild heart will be yours forever.

[*Exit Beatrice.*]

Act 3 Scene 2

A room in Leonato's house.

[*Enter Don John and Borachio.*]

DON JOHN. I've just heard that Claudio, my proud brother's friend, is about to marry Hero. First, they do nothing but boast about their bravery in war, while I'm considered a coward. Now, they've captured everyone's attention with this stupid celebration. How I wish I could destroy their foolish joy.

BORACHIO. You know you can count on me, my lord. I hate Don Pedro and his proud friends as much as you do.

DON JOHN. Claudio is to marry Hero tomorrow. It's too late.

BORACHIO. No, my lord. Trust me, I can ruin their plans.

DON JOHN. How?

BORACHIO. I know one of Hero's servants well. Her name is Margaret. She's quite in love with me, even if I have little time for her.

DON JOHN. Good for you, but how can that help us?

BORACHIO. I'll tell her to look out of Hero's bedroom window tonight at midnight, as I wish to speak to her about our love.

DON JOHN. And so? Where's the trick?

BORACHIO. First, I'll ensure that Hero isn't in her room. Then, I'll ask Margaret to wear something elegant belonging to her mistress Hero. From a distance, she'll look like Hero, and Claudio and your brother will be well tricked.

DON JOHN. What a sharp mind, my friend. I'll make sure that Claudio and my brother are there on time to witness all.

BORACHIO. Yes! With her mistress's clothes, they'll think my Margaret to be Hero, and will be destroyed by her apparent disloyalty.

DON JOHN. I'll go now, and start the doubt in Claudio's mind.

BORACHIO. And I'll prepare Margaret for the part. Sweet, innocent Margaret, who'd rather die than hurt her mistress. I must be careful, so that she suspects nothing.

[*Exit Don John and Borachio.*]

Act 3 Scene 3

Another room in Leonato's house.

[*Enter Don Pedro and Claudio.*]

DON PEDRO. I've just seen Benedick; he looks strange. I think he's in love. And Beatrice?

CLAUDIO. My lord, Hero tells me that she and Ursula played their parts well with her cousin. Now both Benedick and Beatrice love each other dearly, and all sharp words have been replaced with sweet, kindly manners.

DON PEDRO. Good show! Two couples in love! You and Hero, and Beatrice and Benedick.

CLAUDIO. But my lord, isn't that your half-brother Don John coming this way?

DON PEDRO. Yes; he looks as sad as always. Never a smile on his face.

CLAUDIO. I fear he's jealous of you, my lord.

[*Enter Don John.*]

DON JOHN. My lord and brother; I fear there's trouble.

DON PEDRO. What's the matter?

DON JOHN. Please don't hate me when I tell you my sad news, for I know how much you both care about this marriage.

CLAUDIO. If there's a problem, please tell me.

DON JOHN. 'The lady is disloyal.'

CLAUDIO. Who, Hero?

DON JOHN. Yes, Leonato's Hero, your Hero, every man's Hero.

CLAUDIO. Can this be true?

DON PEDRO. I don't believe it.

DON JOHN. Come with me now, and you'll see for yourselves. On the night before her wedding, Hero is standing at her bedroom window, speaking about love to another man.

CLAUDIO. I can't believe you.

DON PEDRO. Me neither, Why such slander[1] of a sweet lady? To break another man's heart?

DON JOHN. There's no slander here. It's midnight; let the evidence speak for itself. Follow me, and see with your own eyes.

CLAUDIO. How sad this happy day has become!

[*Exit all.*]

[*Enter again Don Pedro and Claudio.*]

---

1. **slander:** 誹謗

CLAUDIO [*angrily*]. I never thought to see such a thing tonight. How could Hero do this to me?

DON PEDRO. To betray your love in such a cruel way; I can't believe it.

CLAUDIO. But for sure it was Hero at the window; I even recognised the scarf she wore around her neck; I gave it to her as a gift just a day ago.

DON PEDRO. My lord, you must take revenge, and make her suffer her shame in public.

CLAUDIO. Yes indeed; I'll wait until we're in church tomorrow. Then, I'll tell everyone of her disloyalty.

DON PEDRO. And I'll join you in punishing her, since I encouraged you to love her.

CLAUDIO. How bitter is the taste when sweet love is betrayed.

[*Exit all.*]

Act 4 Scene 1

Inside a church.

[*Enter Don Pedro, Don John, Leonato, Friar Francis, Claudio, Benedick, Hero and Beatrice.*

Claudio and Hero stand next to each other, facing Friar Francis. The others are behind the couple.]

FRIAR FRANCIS [*to Claudio*]. Do you, my lord, come to marry this lady?

CLAUDIO. No.

LEONATO. To be married, Friar, not, to marry. You're the one marrying them.

FRIAR FRANCIS [*to Hero*]. Do you, my lady, come to be married to this gentleman?

HERO. I do.

FRIAR FRANCIS. If anyone knows why you should not be married, then speak now.

CLAUDIO. Hero, do you know any reason why we shouldn't be married?

HERO. No, my lord.

CLAUDIO. Leonato, do you give me your daughter's hand?

LEONATO. She is yours.

CLAUDIO. And what can I give in return?

DON PEDRO. Nothing, unless, you give her back.

CLAUDIO. Thank you dear Prince, for this brilliant suggestion. 'There, Leonato, take her back again.' Look at your daughter. Her red face is evidence of her guilt.

LEONATO. What do you mean, my lord?

CLAUDIO. Not to be married.

HERO. Are you unwell, dear Claudio, that you speak such strange words?

LEONATO. Don Pedro, why don't you speak?

DON PEDRO. What should I say? I'm already guilty of encouraging this hopeless relationship.

LEONATO. Are you serious? Or is this all a bad dream?

DON JOHN. Sir, 'these things are true'.

BENEDICK. This doesn't look like a wedding.

HERO. True!

CLAUDIO. Let me ask you just one question Hero. Who was the man you were talking to last night at your bedroom window?

HERO. I spoke to no man last night.

DON PEDRO. I'm sorry, Leonato, but this is no slander. I, my brother, and poor Claudio saw Hero at midnight last night, talking to a man from her window.

CLAUDIO. Oh Hero! What a Hero you'd have been, if your heart had been true to me. Goodbye forever false love!

[*Hero faints and falls to the ground.*]

BEATRICE. Hero! My dear cousin!

DON JOHN. Come, let's go. All has been said.

[*Exit Don Pedro, Don John and Claudio.*]

BENEDICK. How is the lady?

BEATRICE. Dead, I think! Help, uncle! Hero! Why, Hero? Uncle! Benedick! Friar!

LEONATO. 'Death is the fairest cover for her shame that may be wish'd for.'

BEATRICE. Hero! My poor cousin!

FRIAR. Listen to me; I've been watching this poor unfortunate lady. First, her face was red with shame at the manners of her loved one Claudio; then red turned to white, and a fire lit her eyes, as she silently bore such slander. I firmly believe that those who accuse this sweet lady are doing so unfairly.

LEONATO. Friar, it can't be.

[*Hero opens her eyes.*]

FRIAR. My dear Hero, who's the man they accuse you of seeing?

HERO. Those who accuse me know; I do not.

FRIAR. There's something strange about this story which Don Pedro and Claudio haven't understood.

BENEDICK. They're both men of honour. If there's slander, then it has come from the evil heart of Don John.

LEONATO. I don't know who to believe; but if they're lying about my sweet daughter, I'll kill them with my own hands.

FRIAR. Here's what you should do, my lord, Leonato. Report that Hero is dead. They'll easily believe you, since they saw Hero lying as if dead on the ground. Then, to convince them even more, you must wear black, and pretend to bury her, so that they'll suspect nothing.

LEONATO. But what good will this do?

FRIAR FRANCIS. Claudio's slander will be replaced with guilt for Hero's death. Then he'll regret having accused her. He'll remember her only as good and kind, and her honour will be as before.

BENEDICK. Leonato, listen to the Friar's advice; and even though I love the prince and Claudio, I won't tell them this secret.

FRIAR FRANCIS. Come then, sweet Hero. We'll hide you until all scandal has passed.

[*Exit Friar Francis, Hero and Leonato.*]

BENEDICK. Lady Beatrice, have you been crying all this time?

BEATRICE. Yes, and I'll cry some more.

BENEDICK. I love you more than anything in the world.

BEATRICE. 'I love you with so much of my heart that none is left to protest.'

BENEDICK. My love, what can I do to take away your sadness?

BEATRICE. Kill Claudio.

BENEDICK. Not for the whole wide world!

BEATRICE. Then, you don't love me. I must go.

BENEDICK. Wait, sweet Beatrice. Do you really think Claudio has been unjust to your cousin?

BEATRICE. Yes definitely.

BENEDICK. Enough then. I kiss your hand, and with the same hand I'll challenge Claudio with my sword. Meanwhile, look after your cousin and think of me.

BEATRICE. I will, my love.

[*Exit all.*]

Act 5 Scene 1

Outside Leonato's house.

[*Enter Leonato and Claudio, both with swords.*]

CLAUDIO. Leonato, I'm leaving Messina.

LEONATO. First, listen to what I have to say.

CLAUDIO. I must hurry, Leonato, my lord.

LEONATO [*pulling out his sword*]. Why such a hurry when the damage has been done?

CLAUDIO. Don't quarrel with me, good old man. Put your sword away.

LEONATO. I don't fear you. Claudio, you accused my daughter wrongly and now she's dead. Let me fight you for this slander, for you're to blame for her death.

CLAUDIO. Me, to blame?

LEONATO. I'll prove I'm right with my sword.

CLAUDIO. Away! I will have nothing to do with you.

LEONATO. You've killed my child. Why can't you kill me too?

[*Enter Benedick, sword in hand.*]

BENEDICK. Stop! Leonato, my lord!

CLAUDIO. My dear friend, Benedick. Help this old man to see sense.

BENEDICK. Leonato, let me fight Claudio, for you. I've promised my sweet Beatrice that I'll defend her dead cousin's honour.

CLAUDIO. What words do I hear? First my love betrays me; now my friend!

BENEDICK. He, who lets a sweet lady die of shame, is no friend of mine.

LEONATO. Benedick, my grief makes my heart and body heavy. Fight for me and defeat the enemy.

[*Claudio and Benedick start to fight each other with their swords.*]

[*Enter Don Pedro.*]

DON PEDRO. Stop! I beg you, Claudio, Benedick! Hear my news.

BENEDICK. Speak, my lord, but be quick.

DON PEDRO. Hero was innocent! I've just seen Borachio in prison. He was heard, boasting[1] to a friend. It was all a horrible trick. It wasn't Hero at the window, but her servant Margaret.

CLAUDIO. But why?

DON PEDRO. It was my jealous brother, Don John's plan. He hates us both.

CLAUDIO. Oh sweet Hero! What have I done? Leonato, can you ever forgive me?

LEONATO. If you're really sorry, then you'll agree to do whatever I ask.

CLAUDIO. You're right, my lord. Tell me what I must do.

LEONATO. Tomorrow you'll marry Hero's cousin.

---

1. **boasting:** 自吹自擂

BENEDICK. What? Not Beatrice!

LEONATO. No, another cousin, who's very like Hero, but who you've never seen.

CLAUDIO. Your wish is my command. Come Don Pedro, we must find your brother and make him pay for his crime. Then, tomorrow, I'll pay for mine.

[*Exit Claudio and Don Pedro.*]

BENEDICK. Leonato, what's this plan?

LEONATO. It's right that Claudio should suffer some more. Then, tomorrow, all will become clear. Come now and I'll explain.

[*Exit Benedick and Leonato.*]

Act 5 Scene 2

A room in Leonato's house.

[*Enter Friar Francis, Leonato, Don Pedro, Claudio, Beatrice, Benedick and the unknown bride wearing a mask. Claudio and the bride are standing in front of Friar Francis. Claudio is full of sadness, but ready to carry out Leonato's plan.*]

CLAUDIO [*to bride*]. 'I am your husband, if you like of me.'

UNKNOWN BRIDE [*taking off her mask*]. 'And when I liv'd I was your other wife.'

CLAUDIO. But you're my Hero! My beautiful Hero!

HERO. Yes, my love.

DON PEDRO. Isn't this Hero? Hero that was dead?

LEONATO. 'She died, my lord, but whiles her slander liv'd.'

FRIAR FRANCIS. Can we go now and celebrate the wedding?

BENEDICK. Yes, good Friar, but a double ceremony; for me and Beatrice too will be married.

BEATRICE. Yes my love, a double wedding! You and I, and our Hero and Claudio!

LEONATO. So let's go and get them married, then the dancing can begin.

[*Exit all.*]

Stop & Check

1 **Match the following quotes to the person who said them. Put them in the right order according to the action in the play.**

1 ☐ I am your husband, if you like of me.

2 ☐ The lady is disloyal.

3 ☐ I love you with so much of my heart that none is left to protest.

4 ☐ Death is the fairest cover for her shame that may be wish'd for.

5 ☐ And when I liv'd I was your other wife.

6 ☐ I wish my horse had the speed of your tongue.

A Benedick

B Claudio

C Don John

D Hero

E Beatrice

F Leonato

Grammar for First

2 **Transform the word at the end of each line to complete the sentences about the characters in *Much Ado About Nothing*.**

1 Beatrice is lively and witty, _____ her shy cousin Hero.

LIKE

2 Don Pedro, Claudio and Benedick are famous for their _____ in war.

BRAVE

3 Beatrice is _____ to declare her love to Benedick.

SHAME

4 Benedick realises that his _____ could ruin his chances of love.

PROUD

5 Borachio must be _____, or Margaret may suspect something is wrong.

CARE

6 Friar Francis believes Hero has been _____ accused of betraying Claudio.

FAIR

Speaking

3 **Work in pairs. Talk about the scene you liked best in** *Much Ado About Nothing*. **Here are some ideas to help you:**

- importance of the scene to the play
- characters and setting
- use of surprise, humour, anger, etc.

PRE-READING ACTIVITY

Grammar for First

4 **Read about the next play,** *A Midsummer Night's Dream*. **Decide which answer (A, B, C or D) best fits each gap.**

A Midsummer Night's Dream is one of Shakespeare's most light-hearted plays. It (**1**) _____ the story of two young couples who spend the night in a dark wood where they fall (**2**) _____ the magic powers of the fairies that live there. In the ridiculously short (**3**) _____ of time of just one night, the young couples fall in and out of love, due to the magical tricks of the fairies, before eventually (**4**) _____ a happy ending. Midsummer Night falls on 23rd June, and during Elizabethan (**5**) _____, people believed that flowers picked on this night had magic powers. Young girls also looked (**6**) _____ to this night because it was said that they (**7**) _____dream of their true love. Therefore, on hearing the name of this play, the Elizabethan audience could easily imagine that love, magic and dreams would play an important part in this comedy, which indeed they do.

1	**A** says	**B** tells	**C** asks	**D** gives
2	**A** over	**B** into	**C** below	**D** under
3	**A** length	**B** moment	**C** space	**D** area
4	**A** reaching	**B** arriving	**C** getting	**D** becoming
5	**A** times	**B** day	**C** period	**D** age
6	**A** ahead	**B** for	**C** at	**D** forward
7	**A** are	**B** would	**C** have	**D** did

A Midsummer Night's Dream

Characters:

THESEUS,	Prince of Athens.
EGEUS,	old man; Hermia's father.
HERMIA,	in love with Lysander.
LYSANDER,	in love with Hermia.
DEMETRIUS,	chosen by Egeus to be his daughter's husband.
HELENA,	Hermia's friend. In love with Demetrius.
OBERON,	King of the fairies.
TITANIA,	Queen of the fairies.
PUCK,	one of Oberon's fairies.
MAN IN WOOD,	used by Oberon to trick Titania.

Once there was a law in the city of Athens: a father had the power to force his daughter to marry the man of his choice. If the girl refused to obey her father, she'd die. Since this was a very cruel law, it was hardly ever used. One day however, a very old man, Egeus, came to see Theseus, the Prince of Athens, and demanded that this law be used against his daughter Hermia because she didn't want to marry Demetrius, her father's choice.

Act 1 Scene 1

Athens. The palace of Theseus.

Egeus and his daughter Hermia are standing in front of Theseus, Prince of Athens.

THESEUS. Good Egeus, what news do you bring?

EGEUS. I fear I must complain about my daughter Hermia. I've admired this young gentleman, Demetrius, for a long time, and now I wish him to become my daughter's husband. But Hermia refuses to marry him because another man, Lysander, has stolen her heart. His is not true love, but just a romantic fantasy. I therefore ask you, dear Prince, to judge this case by the law of Athens. If Hermia refuses to marry Demetrius as I wish, then she must die.

THESEUS. What do you say, Hermia? You should respect your father. Demetrius is a handsome gentleman.

HERMIA. So is Lysander.

THESEUS. This is true; but since your father prefers Demetrius, you must choose him.

HERMIA. I wish my father could see Lysander as I see him.

THESEUS. No, you must look with your father's eyes.

HERMIA. I'd rather die than marry Demetrius! What's more my lord, Demetrius once said he loved my dear friend Helena. This sweet lady has lost her heart to him, so surely this is good reason to let me marry Lysander?

THESEUS. This doesn't change your father's wishes; and I can't change the law. So, go now and take time to think; and in four days, give me your answer. Come, Egeus. I must speak to you about my wedding plans.

[*Exit Theseus and Egeus.*]

[*Hermia turns to go but stops as Lysander enters.*]

LYSANDER. My love! Why are you so pale?

HERMIA. Oh Lysander! If I don't obey my father and marry Demetrius, I'll die by Athenian law. But, I'd prefer to die than betray my love for you.

LYSANDER. Don't be afraid my love. History shows us that 'the course of true love never did run smooth.'

HERMIA. Then let's be patient.

LYSANDER. Not for long, my sweet love. I have an aunt who can help us. She lives far from Athens where this cruel law doesn't exist, and where we can get married. Tomorrow night, leave your father's house and run away with me to my aunt's. I'll meet you in the wood not far from the city.

HERMIA. My good Lysander! I promise I'll be there to meet you tomorrow.

LYSANDER. Keep your promise, my love. Now I must go. Look, here comes Helena.

[*Exit Lysander. Enter Helena.*]

HERMIA. Helena, you're beautiful as always.

HELENA. Not beautiful enough for Demetrius who sees only your beauty. Please teach me how to win his heart.

HERMIA. The more I hate, the more he seeks[1] me.

HELENA. The more I love, the more he hates me.

HERMIA. Helena, it's no fault of mine.

HELENA. I know, it's your beauty. I wish I had that fault!

HERMIA. Don't worry Helena; Demetrius will never see me again. I plan to run away from Athens tomorrow night with Lysander. We'll meet in the wood. So, goodbye, my dear sweet friend. And good luck with Demetrius!

[*Exit Hermia.*]

HELENA [speaking to herself]. How happy others can be! Before Demetrius saw Hermia, he declared that he was only mine. Now he won't even look at me! I know, I'll tell him of Hermia's plan.

---

1. **seeks:** 尋找

He'll surely seek Hermia in the wood and be grateful to me.
[*Exit Helena.*]

Act 2 Scene 1

A wood near Athens where Lysander and Hermia will meet that night. This is also the magical wood where tiny fairies live. Oberon the king of the fairies is angry with his queen, Titania, because she refuses to give him a boy as a servant. While Titania, the fairy queen, is walking in the wood, she meets her husband, Oberon.

[*Enter Oberon with his fairy servants; from the other side Titania with her fairies.*]

OBERON. I see in the moonlight, proud Titania.

TITANIA. What, jealous Oberon, is it you? Come my fairies, I wish to avoid this company.

OBERON. Wait! Am I not your lord? Why do you make me angry Titania? Give me the little boy to be my servant.

TITANIA [*angrily*]. I can assure you, no-one will ever take the boy from me. Come, my fairies!

OBERON [*shouting angrily at Titania as she leaves*]. Well, go your way: before daylight I'll make you suffer for this injury.

[*Exit Titania.*]

[*Oberon is very angry and calls for Puck, his most trusted fairy. Puck is clever and always ready to help his king.*]

OBERON. Come here Puck. Fetch me the little purple flower which grows in this wood. The juice of this flower is magic; if dropped on the eyelids[1] of anyone while they're sleeping, it makes them fall in love with the first creature they see on awakening.

PUCK. I'll go now and find it quickly.

[*Exit Puck.*]

OBERON [*speaking to himself*]. I'll use this flower on Titania. While she's sleeping, I'll drop some of its juice on her eyelids. Then,

1. eyelids: 眼瞼

she'll fall in love with the first thing she sees, whether it be a lion or a bear, or even a busy monkey; and I won't break this magic until she agrees to give me her boy as a servant.

[*While Oberon is waiting for Puck, Demetrius and Helena enter the wood. Oberon hides and listens to their conversation.*]

DEMETRIUS [*angrily*]. I don't love you Helena, so stop following me. Where are Lysander and sweet Hermia?

HELENA. I'm drawn to you despite your hard heart. You once said you loved me.

DEMETRIUS. Do I encourage you now? Or, rather, do I not honestly tell you that I don't love you?

HELENA. And even so, I love you all the more.

DEMETRIUS. Don't fill me with anger. I'm sick when I look at you.

HELENA. And I'm sick when I can't see you.

DEMETRIUS. I'll run away from you and leave you to the wild animals in the wood.

[*Demetrius runs away, quickly followed by Helena. The fairy king, Oberon, feels sorry for Helena and her lost love and decides to help her.*]

[*Puck returns.*]

OBERON. Have you got the flower?

PUCK. Yes, here it is.

OBERON. I'll wait until Titania sleeps and drop some of the juice from this flower onto her closed eyes and make her full of horrible fantasies. But Puck, you too must take some of the flower. Look in these woods for a sweet Athenian lady who's in love with an angry young man. Drop some of the love-juice on the man's eyelids while he's sleeping, but ensure that when he awakes, the first thing he sees is the lady.

PUCK. How will I know the man?

OBERON. By his Athenian clothes. Do the task well Puck, then come back to me.

PUCK. Fear not my lord.

[*Exit Puck.*]

[*Enter Titania with her fairies. Oberon hides and watches as his queen prepares for the night and gives her fairies orders.*]

TITANIA. Make sure that the nasty bats don't come near me. But before this, sing me to sleep.

[*The fairies sing, then leave as soon as Titania is asleep on her bed of flowers. Oberon goes near Titania and puts the magic flower-juice on her eyelids.*]

OBERON. What you see when you awake, as your true love you will take.

[*Exit Oberon.*]

Act 2 Scene 2

[*Enter Lysander and Hermia.*]

[*Hermia has escaped from her father's house and meets Lysander in the wood to go to his aunt's. They start walking through the wood in the moonlight.*]

LYSANDER. My love, you look tired: and to tell the truth, I've lost my way. We can rest here if you like, Hermia, until morning.

HERMIA. Kind thought, Lysander: find yourself a bed; I'll sleep on this soft grass.

LYSANDER. Yes, lie down there, my sweet Hermia; I'll lie not far from you, at a respectful distance.

[*They soon fall asleep.*]

[*Enter Puck.*]

[*Puck sees the sleeping couple and thinks they're Demetrius and Helena, the two lovers that Oberon had told him about.*]

PUCK. Who's here? A young man in Athenian clothes, as my master said, and this young lady lying not far away must be the poor girl whose love he refuses. A few drops of love-juice from this magic, purple flower and this young man will love this sweet lady when he awakes and sees her.

[*Puck puts some drops of the magic flower-juice on Lysander's eyelids, then goes to seek Oberon.*]

[*Exit Puck.*]

[*Enter Helena.*]

[*Helena is wandering through the wood seeking Demetrius. She suddenly sees Lysander lying on the ground.*]

HELENA.   But who's here? Lysander! On the ground! Dead? Or asleep? I see no blood, no injury. [*shaking him.*] Lysander if you're alive, then wake up.

[*Lysander opens his eyes and the first thing he sees is Helena. Under the effect of the magic juice, he immediately falls in love with her.*]

LYSANDER.   I'll run through fire for you my sweet Helena. Where's Demetrius? I'll seek him and kill him with my sword so you'll be only mine.

HELENA.   What's this nonsense, Lysander? Be content! You love Hermia and she loves you.

LYSANDER.   Content with Hermia! No; I regret the time I've spent with her. I love you Helena, not Hermia. Before, I was too young to understand true love. Now looking into your eyes, I realise this is where true love lies.

HELENA [*angrily*].   Why does everybody make fun of me? I don't deserve to be treated like this. Isn't it enough that Demetrius won't even look at me? I thought you had a kinder heart than to scorn[1] me in this way.

[*Helena runs away and Lysander follows her, completely forgetting about Hermia who's still asleep.*]

[*Exit Helena and Lysander.*]

[*Hermia wakes up and finds herself alone in the wood.*]

HERMIA.   Lysander! Where are you? Lysander! No sound, no word? Speak to me my love if you can hear me! I feel faint with fear. No answer? Then I'll seek all night long until either I die or I find you.

[*Exit Hermia.*]

---

1. **scorn:** 嘲笑

Act 3 Scene 1

Another part of the wood.

[Demetrius, tired of seeking Hermia, is asleep in the wood. Puck has found Oberon and they're looking at Demetrius lying on the ground.]

OBERON. Ah the Athenian, whose eyes are wet with the flower-juice, is still asleep.

PUCK. But my lord, this is not the same young man I saw. I fear there's another young Athenian wandering in the wood, with the love-juice in his eyes.

OBERON. Well, we must mend this damage.

[Oberon drops some of the love-juice on Demetrius' eyelids then hides with Puck. Demetrius opens his eyes just as Helena reaches the spot where he had been sleeping. She's quickly followed by Lysander. Demetrius looks at Helena; the flower-juice begins to take effect and his words for her are full of love.]

DEMETRIUS. Oh Helena, you're perfect like a goddess, whiter than snow, with lips redder than the sweetest cherries!

HELENA *[angrily]*. You too, Demetrius, want to make fun of me like Lysander! If you were not so arrogant and knew kindness, you wouldn't do me this injury. Isn't it enough that you hate me without joining the others to laugh at me? Both you and Lysander compete for Hermia's love; now there's this new game between you to scorn me.

LYSANDER. Stop this unkindness, Demetrius; I know you love Hermia. I'll give you Hermia if you give me Helena whom I'll love till my death.

HELENA. I've never heard such nonsense!

DEMETRIUS. Lysander, you can keep Hermia. If ever I loved her, all that love has gone.

My heart has returned to Helena and there it will remain.

[Just then Hermia, who has been seeking Lysander, arrives on the scene.]

HERMIA. Lysander! At last my love, I've found you; but why did you leave me all alone?

LYSANDER. There was no reason to stay when love called me elsewhere.

HERMIA. What love called you elsewhere?

LYSANDER. Sweet Helena, who lights the night with her beauty. Why do you keep following me, Hermia? Don't you realise that hate made me leave you?

HERMIA. You can't mean what you say.

HELENA [*angrily*]. So, you too, Hermia, wish to scorn me! All three of you against me! How can you be so cruel Hermia? All the time we've spent together; you were like a sister to me.

HERMIA. Your words shock me. I'm not making fun of you; but you of me!

HELENA. So why suddenly does Demetrius call me his love? And why does Lysander show affection for me in front of you? It's because you're part of this cruel game to scorn me!

HERMIA. I don't understand.

HELENA. Enough of your false, sad glances and talking behind my back, all three of you! If you had any pity, you wouldn't scorn me like this.

LYSANDER. Helena stay calm! My love, my life, my soul!

HELENA [*angrily*]. Ha! Excellent!

HERMIA. Lysander, stop this cruel joke!

DEMETRIUS. Helena, I love you more than Lysander does.

LYSANDER. Then we must fight for her!

HERMIA. Lysander; what are you saying? [*Hermia tries to pull Lysander to her.*]

LYSANDER. Leave me alone, Hermia!

DEMETRIUS. Come, Lysander. We'll seek a place in the wood to fight, and whoever wins will have the love of Helena as his prize.

[*Exit Demetrius and Lysander.*]

HELENA. I will no longer stay to be scorned by you, Hermia. I'll run after my Demetrius to see that no harm comes to him.

[*Exit Helena.*]

HERMIA. I'm amazed and don't know what to say.

[*Exit Hermia.*]

[*Oberon, the fairy king, and Puck had been listening to their quarrels.*]

OBERON. This is all your fault, Puck.

PUCK. Believe me, my king, it was a mistake; didn't you tell me that I should recognise the Athenian man by his clothes? Well that's what I did; only it was the wrong Athenian… anyway, it's all quite fun to watch!

OBERON. You heard that Demetrius and Lysander have gone to seek a place to fight. We must stop them; you must cover the wood in a thick fog so that these two young men can't find each other. When they've walked so long that they can walk no more, they'll lie and sleep. Then you'll drop the juice of this other flower onto Lysander's eyelids, and when he awakes he'll forget his new love for Helena and return to his old passion for Hermia. Demetrius will continue to love Helena and all that has happened will seem just a dream. Go quickly Puck. I must see what my sweet love, Titania, has found.

[*Exit Oberon.*]

PUCK. Up and down, up and down I'll lead them until they drop.

[*Exit Puck.*]

Act 3 Scene 2

[*Titania is still sleeping. Near her there's a man from the village who has fallen asleep after losing his way in the wood. Oberon puts a donkey's head over the man's head; with his magic it fits perfectly. He's very pleased with himself.*]

OBERON [*laughing*]. This man with the donkey's head will be my Titania's true love.

[*He hides and watches the scene.*]

[*The man wakes up, not realising that he now has the head of a donkey, and walks over to where Titania is sleeping. Titania opens her eyes slowly and sees the man with the donkey's head; the flower-juice starts to take effect.*]

TITANIA. 'What angel wakes me from my flowery bed?' Are you as wise as you are handsome?

MAN. I'm neither. I wish only to find my way out of this wood.

TITANIA. Please, don't go. I have great powers. Stay with me, and my fairies will be your servants.

[*The man seems pleased with the idea of fairy servants and decides to stay.*]

TITANIA. My fairies, be kind to this gentleman; feed him with peaches and grapes, and steal honey for him from the bees. [*to the man.*] Come and sit with me so I may kiss your long hairy ears, my love.

MAN. Now, please don't disturb me as I wish to sleep.

TITANIA. Sleep then my love, and I'll hold you in my arms. Oh, how I love you!

[*Once the man is sleeping, Oberon comes out of his hiding-place.*]

OBERON. What do I see, Titania? Are you in love with this monster, half man, half donkey?

TITANIA [*ashamed*]. I don't understand why I'm attracted to this strange love. Please forgive me my fairy king.

OBERON. You abandon your honour with your choice of love; but if you truly wish my respect once more, then give me your boy as my servant.

TITANIA. I will readily give you the boy if you promise not to tell anyone of my strange love.

OBERON. I forgive you, my fairy queen. Now rest with your dear monster and fear not my anger.

[*Titania sleeps once more; Oberon, delighted that he has the boy, decides to undo the magic. He drops the juice from another flower onto Titania's eyelids to bring her back to normal. Then he takes the donkey's head off the man and leaves him sleeping.*]

OBERON. Wake up my Titania, my sweet queen, and remember all that has happened as if only in a dream.

TITANIA. My Oberon! What a strange dream; I thought I was in love with a donkey!

OBERON. Come my queen, all is well now. But before Theseus is married tomorrow, we must seek the two young Athenian couples and solve their love problems.

TITANIA. I don't know these stories of trouble with love, but you can tell me as we search for them in the wood.

[*Exit Oberon and Titania.*]

Act 4 Scene 1

[*Lysander, Demetrius, Hermia and Helena are lying sleeping on the ground. After wandering through the dark, foggy wood all night, clever Puck manages to lead the four lovers, one by one, to a green space among the trees. There, unaware of each other, they all fall asleep, exhausted.*]

[*Enter Puck.*]

PUCK [*putting the juice on Lysander's eyelids*]. Sleep peacefully while I give you the solution to your love troubles, Lysander. When you awake, you'll love dear Hermia once more, leaving Demetrius and Helena to share their love; so every man will have his own.

[*Titania and Oberon arrive and without being seen, watch happily as the young lovers awake and find happiness again. Suddenly, they hear the sound of horses in the distance. Theseus and Egeus have come to seek Hermia.*]

[*Enter Theseus and Egeus.*]

THESEUS. Good morning, friends. Weren't you afraid to sleep near your enemy in love, Lysander?

LYSANDER. Sir, I don't remember very well how I got here. Ah yes, I wanted to escape with Hermia to avoid the cruelty of Athenian law.

EGEUS. Enough! Demetrius, he wants to steal your future wife!

DEMETRIUS. Sir, Helena told me of their plan; I came to look for them in the wood, but since then, my love for Hermia has melted like snow; now, the only one I love is Helena.

THESEUS. If this is the case, then Egeus let these happy couples be free to marry as love has joined them; Lysander and Hermia; Demetrius and Helena.

EGEUS. So be it, my lord.

[*Exit Theseus, Egeus and the happy couples.*]

PUCK [*to the audience*]. 'If we shadows have offended,
Think but this, and all is mended,
That you have but slumbered here
While these visions did appear.'

[*Exit Puck.*]

Stop & Check

1 **Answer the questions about *A Midsummer Night's Dream*. Support your answers with evidence from the play.**

1 Why is Egeus angry at the start of the play?

2 Why does Helena decide to tell Demetrius about Hermia's plan to escape with Lysander?

3 Who is Oberon angry with at the start of Act 2 and why?

4 What mistake does Puck make and what are the consequences?

5 How does Helena react to Lysander's words of love?

6 What happens to Titania?

7 How does Puck solve the problems he has caused?

8 At the end, Puck talks about dreaming. On what other occasions is this idea mentioned in the play?

Writing

2a **Which character did you like best in *A Midsummer Night's Dream*? Write a paragraph describing the character and giving reasons for your choice.**

_____

_____

_____

_____

_____

2b **Who said: 'The course of true love never did run smooth'? Explain what it means and how true it is for the play.**

_____

_____

_____

_____

_____

Vocabulary

3a **Complete the table with the missing words. They can all be found in the play.**

Noun	Adjective
1	powerful
cruelty	**2**
anger	**3**
truth	**4**
5	beautiful
6	unkind
patience	**7**
arrogance	**8**

3b **Complete the sentences with a noun or adjective from the table.**

1 Hermia promised Lysander that she would be _____ and not lose all hope of marrying him.
2 Helena was very jealous of Hermia's _____.
3 Egeus is convinced that Hermia can only find _____ love with Demetrius.
4 Theseus has no _____ to protect Hermia from Athenian law.

Speaking

4 **Some people say: 'love is blind'. Talk in pairs:**

- Discuss how Shakespeare makes use of this belief in *A Midsummer Night's Dream?*
- Decide if you agree or disagree with this statement, giving reasons.
- Discuss the importance given to appearance in modern society.

Charles Lamb (1775-1834)
Mary Lamb (1764-1847)

In 1807, Charles and Mary Lamb wrote their book *Tales from Shakespeare* for children. The plays were written as stories, and were made simpler and more suitable for the younger reader by concentrating only on the main story-line. The Lambs used Shakespeare's own words whenever possible, and changed them only when they thought them to be too old-fashioned or difficult to understand for children. They divided the work between them, with Mary writing the comedies, while her brother Charles wrote the tragedies.

Family Life and Tragedy

Mary Lamb was born in London on 3rd December, 1764, and was the third of seven children. Her brother, Charles, was born on 10th February, 1775, and was the youngest of the family. Apart from Mary and Charles, only their eldest brother, John, survived childhood. Charles and Mary had a close relationship all their lives and, as a young girl, Mary taught her younger brother to read. Through their father, who worked as an assistant to Samuel Salt, a member of the government, Charles and Mary learned about literature and had the chance of meeting many famous writers of that time. Apart from being writers, Mary worked as a dressmaker, while her brother, Charles, worked with the British East India Trading Company. Unfortunately, the family began to have both money and health problems. Mary continued working as a dressmaker, but also had to look after her parents who were both ill, as well as her elder brother who had had an accident. Due to all this pressure, in 1796, she had a mental breakdown, and during a furious argument, killed her mother. Charles stood by his sister, and with the help of friends, managed to avoid his sister being kept in prison for the rest of her life. For a while, she lived in a village called Hackney, not far from London. Then, after their father died, Charles brought his sister back to London to live with him. Charles and Mary had been close since childhood and at this point in his life, Charles took full responsibility for his sister Mary, who was often in and out of hospital due to her illness. Neither of them ever married, and were together till Charles' death in 1834.

Success

During their time together, and despite Mary's illness, Charles and his sister formed a social circle whose main interest was literature, and which included famous poets like Wordsworth and Coleridge. Charles had gone to school with Coleridge who was probably his oldest and best friend, and had some of his poems included in a book by Coleridge called *'Poems on Various Subjects'*, published in 1796. His biggest success however, was *'Tales from Shakespeare'* which his sister helped him to write. Their life became easier as they were now wealthier, even if Mary, who had always worked hard all her life, found it hard to give orders to servants in her own home.

Task

Complete this form about Mary Lamb.

Date of birth: _____

Place of birth: _____

Brothers' names: _____

Professions: _____

Crime: _____

Illness: _____

Book: _____

Date of death: _____

The Elizabethan Age (CLIL History)

The Elizabethan Age, often known as the Golden Age, was a period of new ideas and new learning. It was the English Renaissance, and the English were proud of their nation and were full of hope for the future. Schools began studying Latin and Greek, and students were encouraged to develop their own ability to ask questions and, through reason, find the answers themselves. It was also an age of exploration which brought many new words to the English language. Books appeared in prose about new places, business, and manners, and were in great demand by the public. Poetry, music and the theatre were all popular during this time as well.

Queen Elizabeth I (1533-1603)

Elizabeth was the daughter of Henry VIII and Anne Boleyn and was born on 7th September 1533. Her mother, Anne, was executed when Elizabeth was just two years old. From then, she was cared for by servants, as her father, Henry VIII, was too busy with his new wife and family. After a hard young life, she eventually became queen in 1558 and ruled England for 45 years until her death in 1603. She never married and was the last of the Tudor Dynasty. She was a tolerant queen and was moderate both with her government and religious matters. She was also well-educated and loved drama, especially plays by Marlowe and Shakespeare. She became very popular with her people who trusted her good judgement. The people of that time were interested in human nature and passion but, at the same time, needed a strong leader to keep chaos from their lives and give them a sense of order.

The Golden Age of Exploration

At the beginning of this great period of exploration, the Spanish and the Portuguese ruled the seas and made their countries rich by bringing gold and silver from the New World. However, Queen Elizabeth I encouraged progress in science and building, and soon England was making ships that were stronger and faster than any others at sea. This led to great success in exploration and brought much wealth to England, which began to buy and sell from countries like India and China and started also to settle in America.

Sir Francis Drake (1540-1596)

Francis Drake was born in Devonshire, England, and was the eldest of twelve sons. At first, he became famous as a seaman, explorer and pirate who attacked Spanish ships and stole their gold and silver. He was encouraged to do this by Elizabeth and, in 1577, was chosen by the queen to sail around the world on his ship the *Golden Hind*. He was successful and claimed what is now San Francisco as English land, before returning home in 1580. It was then that he became Sir Francis, for services to his country. He also played an important role in defeating the Spanish Armada in the English Channel in 1588, when the Spanish tried to attack England.

Sir Walter Raleigh (c. 1554-1618)

Another famous explorer of that time was Walter Raleigh. He too was born in Devonshire and was a distant relative of Sir Francis Drake. He first sailed to America in 1578 on his ship *The Falcon*. Queen Elizabeth enjoyed his company and he soon became one of her favourites. He was also a brilliant poet and created the secret society called *The School of Night,* where new ideas and beliefs were discussed with other important members of Elizabethan society. In 1584, the queen allowed him to explore North America, and a few months later, he settled in a place he called Virginia, in North Carolina. This colony did not survive for long, but it was the start of the English colonies in the New World.

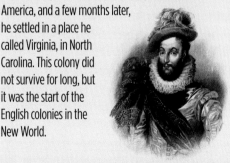

Task

Internet search

Have a look on the internet. Find out more about the Elizabethan Age.

What progress was there in science?

How was the education system organised?

What was the life of women like?

What did people eat in those days?

SYLLABUS 語法重點和學習主題

Verbs:

present perfect continuous	used to
past perfect continuous	phrasal verbs
future perfect	all passive forms
third conditional	wish
make, get, let, have something done	conditionals with may/might

Modal verbs:

May, might

Answer Key 答案

///

Tales from Shakespeare

Page 9
1 **1** the **2** where **3** him **4** due **5** most **6** were **7** like **8** age **9** from
10 between **11** of **12** makes

Page 10
2 **1** monologue **2** asides **3** stage directions **4** soliloquy **5** turning point **6** plot
3 Answers may vary
4 **1** F France was divided into kingdoms, each ruled by a prince.
2 T
3 F It is the name of the forest he lives in.
4 F They are cousins.
5 T
6 F She is not enthusiastic about it.

Page 28
1 **Across** **1** chain **3** poem **6** sword **7** handkerchief **8** uncle
Down **1** cottage **2** wedding **4** France **5** forest **6** snake

Page 29
2 **1** wasn't allowed to **2** loved Sir Rowland except **3** had no chance of winning
4 has not seen Rosalind since **5** too tired and hungry to
3 **1** Because in the past when he visited her, Portia's eyes sent him messages of love.
2 Her father died and left her all his fortune.
3 So he can dress elegantly and try to win Portia's heart by buying her many gifts.
4 Antonio has no money at the moment, because he is waiting for his three ships to arrive in Venice.
5 Bassanio can't wait because another man may steal Portia's heart.
6 They will find somebody to borrow the money from and Antonio will take care of all costs.

Page 46
1 **1** B **2** C **3** B **4** A **5** B **6** B **7** B
2 **1** Bassanio; When he comes to visit and she says she wants to be his wife.
2 Later in the story the ring is used as a comic device; Portia and Nerissa play a joke on Bassanio and Gratiano. First they make them give their rings away, then they accuse them of having broken their promise.

Page 47
3 **1** begged **2** spoils **3** deny **4** didn't deserve **5** lacked **6** had insulted **7** didn't trust
4 **1** most **2** both **3** who **4** to **5** had **6** back **7** well **8** falls **9** being

Page 63
1 **1** F Duke of Milan. **2** F 12 years. **3** T **4** F The spirit, Ariel appears to them in the form of a terrifying bird. **5** F He decides to forgive them because he says if a spirit like Ariel can feel pity, then he, as a human being, should too. **6** T **7** F He buries his books at the end.
2 **1** keen **2** looked **3** made **4** because **5** apart **6** approved **7** betrayed

Page 64

3a Possible answers:

At first, Miranda seems really young and totally under the control of her father. They have been on the island for 12 years and only now he decides to tell her about her past. She trusts him completely. She worries that she may have caused her father problems when she was little. Prospero is kind to his daughter, but also in complete control of her. He decides to change her fate, by causing the storm, so letting her meet Ferdinand. Since she has never seen any other man, apart from her father, it is more than likely that she will fall in love with Ferdinand as her father hopes. In her meeting with Ferdinand, we see Miranda's innocent, sweet nature. She is open and doesn't try to hide her feelings, even if she worries about not following her father's advice not to speak too much.

This is the first time she makes a decision when she decides to marry Ferdinand without even asking her father, but at the same time, we know that she is doing exactly what her father wants as usual. Even at the end she is still in wonder at all the new people she sees and thinks that they are all handsome. Although during these twelve years, her father has taught her many things, she is not used to the outside world, and we can think that in her future life in Naples, she will again be controlled by a man, this time Ferdinand. I like her / don't like her because....................

4 Answers may vary.

Page 82

1 1C 2F **3**A **4**B **5**G **6**J **7**H **8**D **9**I **10**E

2a Possible answer:

The triangle is made up of Orsino, Olivia and Viola. Orsino loves Olivia, Olivia loves Cesario who is really Viola, and Viola loves Orsino.

Disguise is very important because, if Viola hadn't dressed up as a boy, Olivia wouldn't have fallen in love with her; but at the same time, because of this disguise Olivia marries Sebastian and finds love in the end.

In the end Viola reveals she is a girl so she can marry Orsino and Olivia is happy to be married to Sebastian.

2b Personal answers.

Page 83

3 **1** wouldn't have sunk **2** says **3** weren't **4** hadn't lent **5** had Sebastian started **6** has been writing **7** wouldn't have been arrested **8** would give

4 **1** battle **2** crime **3** murder **4** strike **5** blood **6** evil

Page 102

1 **1** He meets 3 witches.

2 It is vitally important because it is the start of Macbeth's desire to become king. His subsequent actions are a consequence of this ambition to make the witches' prediction come true.

3 His first victim is the King of Scotland, Duncan, as killing him is the only way Macbeth can hope to become king.

4 Banquo's ghost appears to Macbeth when he is having supper with his lords.

5 At the beginning, Lady Macbeth seems more evil and determined than her husband and encourages him to murder Duncan. However by the end of the play she has gone mad with guilt, and imagines her hands dirty with blood. In the end she dies.

6 The witches' prediction about Birnam Wood moving comes true because Malcolm tells all his men to take a branch from a tree and walk hiding behind it, so from far away it looked as if the trees were moving.

7 Malcolm, Duncan's eldest son becomes King of Scotland at the end of the play.

2 **1** At the start of the play, the Norwegians had been defeated by the Scottish army.
2 Macbeth was thanked by King Duncan for his bravery in battle.
3 Macbeth will be encouraged by Lady Macbeth to carry out his evil plan.
4 Lady Macbeth was given a diamond by the king for her kindness.
5 Banquo has been invited by Macbeth to a special dinner.
6 Dinner is being served when Banquo's ghost appears.
7 While Banquo was being attacked by the murderers, his son ran away.
8 Macbeth used to be admired and respected.
9 The servants will be marked by Macbeth with Duncan's blood.
10 The spirits will be called by the witches for Macbeth.

Page 103
3a Personal answer.
3b Personal answers.
4 **1**F Hero is Leonato's daughter.   **2**T   **3**F They always argue with each other.
   4F He is secretly watching Hero.   **5**F Leonato disagrees with his opinion.   **6**T

Page 120
1 **1**B   **2**C   **3**E   **4**F   **5**D   **6**A
2 **1** unlike   **2** bravery   **3** ashamed   **4** pride   **5** careful   **6** unfairly

Page 121
3 Answers may vary.
4 **1**B   **2**D   **3**C   **4**A   **5**A   **6**D   **7**B

Page 136
1 **1** He wants Hermia to marry Demetrius but she refuses.
2 To win his favour.
3 He is angry with his wife Titania because she doesn't want to give him a boy servant.
4 He mistakes Lysander for Demetrius and puts the magic love juice in his eyes, so instead of Demetrius, Lysander falls in love with Helena.
5 She is angry, because she thinks he is making fun of her.
6 She falls in love with a donkey, because Oberon puts the love juice in her eyes.
7 He makes sure Demetrius and Lysander don't meet to fight. Then when all the couples are sleeping he puts another juice in Lysander's eyes so that he will love Hermia once more.
8 It is mentioned when Oberon tells Titania to dream for example.
2a Answers may vary.
2b Lysander said this. It is true because before eventually coming to a happy ending, the couples have lots of problems.

Page 137
3a

Noun	Adjective
1 power	powerful
cruelty	**2** cruel
anger	**3** angry
truth	**4** true
5 beauty	beautiful
6 unkindness	unkind
patience	**7** patient
arrogance	**8** arrogant

3b **1** patient   **2** beauty   **3** true   **4** power
4 Open answer

Page 139

Date of birth: 3rd December 1764
Place of birth: London
Brothers' names: Charles and John
Professions: writer, dressmaker
Crime: she killed her mother
Illness: mental breakdown
Book: Tales of Shakespeare – she wrote the comedies.
Date of death: 1847

Page 141

Answers may vary.

© 2016, licensed by ELI Edizioni, Italy

Read for Pleasure: *Tales from Shakespeare* 莎翁故事集

作　　者：Charles and Mary Lamb
改　　寫：Silvana Sardi
繪　　畫：Alicia Baladan
照　　片：Shutterstock
責任編輯：傅薇
封面設計：涂慧
出　　版：商務印書館（香港）有限公司
　　　　　香港筲箕灣耀興道 3 號東滙廣場 8 樓
　　　　　http://www.commercialpress.com.hk
發　　行：香港聯合書刊物流有限公司
　　　　　香港新界荃灣德士古道 220-248 號荃灣工業中心 16 樓
印　　刷：中華商務彩色印刷有限公司
　　　　　香港新界大埔汀麗路 36 號中華商務印刷大廈 14 字樓
版　　次：2022 年 5 月第 1 版第 3 次印刷
　　　　　© 2016 商務印書館（香港）有限公司
　　　　　ISBN 978 962 07 0480 2
　　　　　Printed in Hong Kong
　　　　　版權所有　不得翻印